A FAMILY FOR CHRISTMAS
WILLOW PARK

NOELLE ADAMS

CHAPTER 1

LYDIA TOOK TEN DEEP BREATHS IN A ROW.

When she was still so angry she wanted to scream, she took ten more deep breaths before pulling her car out of the church parking lot and heading for the interstate.

She'd only calmed down slightly when she grabbed her phone and connected to Daniel, the pastor of her hometown church, who was always her first call after a meeting as frustrating as the one she'd just had.

It rang four times, and Lydia was about to hang up, realizing it was Sunday afternoon and Daniel was probably resting.

Before she could disconnect, he answered the phone. "Hey, Lydia."

"Hi," she said, feeling even guiltier since he sounded kind of distracted. "Sorry to call on a Sunday afternoon. I should have waited until tomorrow."

"It's fine. Jessica and I were just cleaning up from lunch." He paused as if he were briefly searching his memory. "You were visiting another church this morning?"

1

"Yeah. In Charlotte."

"I guess it didn't go well then."

"The presentation and Sunday school hour went great but not the meeting with the Session." She paused to take another deep breath, reliving again her frustration from the meeting she'd just had with the elders of the church.

"What happened?" Daniel asked.

"Why the hell doesn't anyone think I can do legal work in India without being married? How exactly is a husband supposed to be necessary for me to work with trafficked women?"

She was exaggerating a little since the NGO she was planning to work with was fine with her being a single woman. But she needed to raise support for her salary and expenses since the Christian human rights organization wasn't able to give her a salary yet. That meant asking for money from individuals and churches. The churches in her circle always had money in their budgets for mission work, which is how they would classify her plan to work toward rescuing and restoring girls and women forced into the sex trade, but her Presbyterian denomination was a small and conservative one, which was making her attempt to raise support more difficult than it should have been.

She'd been at it for eight months now, and she wasn't even close to having the yearly pledges she needed.

"You know," she went on, "one of the elders asked me today why I wanted to do this instead of getting married and starting a family."

She was venting, and she sounded too frustrated, so she tried to dial it back. "Sorry. You've heard all this before. I'll call back tomorrow so you can enjoy your afternoon."

"Are you headed for Columbia now?"

"Yeah. I'm not sure it's going to be worth my time since it's such a huge missions conference, which means I'm not going to get much attention. But I'll give it a try."

"Try not to exude impatience with people. They can pick up on it."

She bit back her reply, which would have been neither patient nor gentle. She had always been an honest, straightforward person—some people would call her too much so—but as she'd gotten older she'd learned to temper those qualities with courtesy.

For the most part.

But it wasn't like she'd be snapping at the church elders from whom she was asking money.

"I'm doing my best," she gritted.

"I know. Sorry. I know you're in a tough position. Hey, when you're in Columbia tonight, you might touch base with Gabe Alexander. I was talking to him last week, and he'll be at that same conference this evening. You two have a lot in common."

"Who is this?" She'd reached the on-ramp for I-77, so she pulled her car onto the interstate, heading south.

"Gabe Alexander. You remember him, don't you? He was in Willow Park one summer several years back."

Lydia felt flustered and distracted from her aggravating morning, but she tried to search her memory for that name. "Maybe."

"It was the summer the Johnsons were visiting from India. He heard their testimony too and felt called to India just like you did. You really need to connect with him." Daniel's tone changed as if he were just making a connection in his mind. "I don't know why I didn't think about it before. I'll text you his phone number. Promise me you'll talk to him this evening."

"Okay. I promise." She had no idea why Daniel sounded so excited, but she had no reason not to look the guy up. "Wait, is he Mary and Henry's son? From church? I think I remember their son if it's him. He and his wife had a new baby that summer, didn't they? I took care of her in the nursery some and babysat for them once. They paid really well."

She didn't know why she added the last bit since it was irrelevant, but she remembered it, so she said it.

She usually said what she thought.

"Yeah. That's him."

"So they're going to India too?"

"He is. They're not married anymore."

"Oh. Okay. Sure, I'll talk to him."

"I think it would be really worth your time." Daniel paused before he added in a different tone. "Jessica is giving me the sign to hang up. Call me tomorrow at the office if you want. Let me know how it goes tonight."

"Okay. Will do. Thanks."

Lydia hung up and stared out at the highway in front of her.

Since that summer when she was eighteen and she'd met the missionaries from India who were visiting Willow Park, she'd known what she wanted to do with her life. Work with children and women caught in sex trafficking. She'd made two trips to India in college and then two more during the summers she was in law school working with the legal team at the organization she was planning to work with now full-time.

She was sure this was what God wanted her to do, and it just didn't seem right that something so trivial was standing in her way.

So she was a single woman. She was still capable of doing good work in India.

What was wrong with people anyway?

Maybe she was intrinsically different than other women she knew, but she'd never felt a strong urge to get married and have children. She'd had crushes on guys before—sure. She'd dated several different guys through college and in the two years she'd worked in an office after she'd graduated. But once she'd started law school, fewer guys had asked her out, and she'd started to focus more and more on what she wanted to do with her life.

Marriage just wasn't as important as what she could do in India. She was absolutely convinced of it now.

She'd dreamed of working in India for the past several years, the way some women dreamed of a wedding day. She was so close now, and she was going to finally get there—whether she was married or not.

When she got to Columbia, it was midafternoon, and she called Gabe Alexander from her car.

They had a brief, slightly awkward conversation while she explained who she was and why she was calling him out of the blue.

When she told him that Daniel said they should touch

base, Gabe suggested they meet for coffee at five, an hour before the missions conference began.

That sounded good to Lydia since she'd been thinking they'd have to meet afterward, which would put her drive back to Willow Park even later.

She only had vague memories of the man. She'd been eighteen—at home for the summer after her freshman year in college. Mr. Alexander and his wife were just a new couple at the church with a newborn baby.

He'd come across as quiet, intelligent, and always busy —even when she'd been over to babysit, and he and his wife had been on their way for an evening out. His wife had been charming and stylish. She'd seemed maybe a little superficial.

Lydia hadn't known them well, but they'd seemed happy enough. She wondered why they'd gotten divorced.

The girl must be nine now.

Lydia and Gabe arranged to meet at a coffee shop near the church. She had some trouble finding a parking space, so she was running about five minutes late when she walked in.

She stood at the entrance and looked around, hoping she'd recognize him when she saw him.

Almost immediately her eyes landed on a man sitting alone in a corner. He wore a suit, but his dress shirt was unbuttoned, and he wasn't wearing a tie. He had medium brown hair and broad shoulders and a slightly heavy-lidded gaze, making him look tired... and kind of sexy.

She wasn't sure where that thought had even come from, but she was sure this was Gabe Alexander. She walked over to him.

His eyes widened, and he stood up as she approached.

"Lydia?" he asked.

"Yes." She reached a hand out toward him. "It's nice to see you again. It's been a long time."

"It has." He shook her hand, his grip strong and very warm. Then they both sat down at the small table. "I'm not sure I would have recognized you."

She gave a half shrug. She didn't think she looked that much different now than she had back then. She still had shoulder-length dark reddish hair, green eyes, and a tall figure. She worked out regularly, so she was in decent shape—although not as fit as she'd been in college when she'd swum competitively. She was dressed more maturely than she used to be since she was now wearing one of her normal church-visit outfits. Long, flared skirt, a fitted jacket, and tall leather boots.

But still she didn't think she looked all that different.

"Can I get you a coffee or something?" he asked, gesturing toward the counter.

She saw he didn't have anything to drink yet, so she nodded. "Sure. Just black coffee. Thanks."

She watched him as he went up to the counter to order their drinks. She saw other women watching him too.

He really was very good-looking, with a kind of understated power in his stance and expression, like he was accommodating the world to go on as it liked until he decided differently. But when he put his foot down, the world would listen.

It was a strange sort of response to such a brief meeting. Irrational really, since he hadn't done anything but shake her hand and get up to get them coffee. Probably a sign that Lydia needed to catch up on her sleep.

Since there was a line waiting to pick up ordered drinks, he came back and took his seat again after he'd ordered. He asked, "So Daniel thought we should connect?"

"Yeah. He said we have a lot in common since I'm working on raising support to get to Bangalore. So you're trying to get to India too?"

He nodded. "I've been working with the business center in Bangalore for eight years now—making a two-week trip every year. Now there's a codirector position open that I want to take."

"What does the business center do?"

"It provides training, resources, and mentoring for people trying to start businesses in India who need some extra help or support." He leaned back in his seat and looked at her with half-closed eyes. "It's a great ministry, really helping people get their businesses going."

"Well, that sounds great. You started your own business here, didn't you?" One thing Lydia remembered from back then was that the Alexanders had a lot of money, at least by Willow Park standards.

"Yeah. Medical supplies."

The way he said it was understated, as if his company weren't that big a deal. But it was evidently really success-ful. She was about to ask a question when she noticed something up at the counter.

Frowning, she said, "Are our coffees ready?"

He glanced up casually. "Doesn't look like it."

"Well, that girl was behind you in line, and she already got hers."

"What does it matter?"

She was faintly annoyed at his disinterest, but she knew that feeling wasn't rational. So she made herself relax. "Well, it doesn't matter a lot. But generally people get their stuff in the correct order."

When she turned back to him, she saw he was watching her face with a mingling of interest and amusement.

"What?" she asked.

"Nothing." He was smiling for real now, and it was so attractive she momentarily lost her breath. "It's just coffee."

"I know it's just coffee. But I think people should be served in the right order." She gave him a sheepish smile. "Patience isn't my virtue."

"I can see that."

She was going to respond to his teasing, but she saw their drinks finally get set on the counter, so she jumped up to get them.

He was still smiling as he watched her walk back to the table. She wasn't sure what to make of the expression in his eyes.

Then she realized they should get down to business since the missions conference would be starting in forty minutes. "You were telling me about the business center," she prompted.

"Yes. It's a great ministry, and I really think they could use my experience." He shook his head and let out a long breath.

"So what's the problem?"

He gave her a dry half smile. "My problem is I don't have a wife."

She gasped and straightened up, suddenly realizing

what Daniel had seen they had in common. "Seriously? So you're having problems raising support?"

"No. I'm rolling in support. I don't even really need it since I've got more than enough income on my own."

Lydia tried very hard not to resent this leisurely declaration, when it was like pulling teeth for her to get even the smallest of pledges.

He continued, "The problem is the mission organization that runs the center. They keep hesitating since they're not sure I'm in an appropriate 'domestic situation' for the role of codirector."

"They really think you need to be married to do the work? I thought it was just women who were blessed with those concerns."

"I think they're okay with me being single. They're not okay with me being a single father."

"Oh." She thought about that. "So you have custody of your daughter? What was her name? Eleanor?"

"Yeah. Ellie. I have full custody. This is evidently a problem." He sounded almost lazy, but she recognized a faint bitterness in his eyes, one that told her he was just as frustrated with his situation as she was with hers.

"And they don't think, since you're able to work out the care of your daughter here, you'll be able to handle it there too?"

"I guess not. I'm not even going to be in India year-round. I'll stay here for the school year and then just go over there for the summers. I can make other short trips during the year as needed and do a lot of the work virtually anyway. I'm moving back to Willow Park so my folks can help out more in watching Ellie when I have to make the shorter trips. But they're not all convinced."

She gave him a sympathetic smile. "We're kind of in reverse situations then. My organization is fine with me not being married, but I can't raise the support I need because the churches don't think I should be gallivanting around the world when I could be staying here and having babies."

He raised his eyebrows. "Is it really that bad? So what exactly would you be doing?"

She sighed. "Maybe I'm exaggerating. But I'm having a lot of trouble raising support. I'd be working with the legal team. The organization does investigation and provides legal assistance for underaged girls in brothels, trying to rescue them and then give them the help they need to get reoriented afterward. I can't practice law there, of course, but I can work with the Indian lawyers. There are laws in India against a lot of the sex trafficking—the laws just aren't always enforced. Anyway, there's really important work to do, and I think I can help. But everyone's worried that I can't do it for some reason as an unmarried woman."

"There are plenty of single, professional women in India."

"I know. I've heard it justified so many ways it makes me want to scream, but not very many churches want to support me."

His eyes were so dark a blue they almost looked violet, and they were sympathetic at the moment as they gazed at her. "No wonder Daniel said we should talk."

"Yeah. If only we could somehow pool resources." She

gave a huff. "I need financial support, which you have more than enough of. And you need…"

"A wife." The one word was drawled as if in jest.

But after a pregnant pause, both of them stiffened. Their eyes flew up to meet in an odd moment of complete understanding.

They were basically strangers, but she knew—without doubt—that they'd both had the same bizarre idea at the exact same time.

After a minute, Gabe put down his coffee, which he'd been holding frozen halfway to his mouth. "No, it's crazy."

"Yeah," she said, letting out a breath and feeling ridiculously deflated. For a moment it was like all of her prayers had been miraculously answered. "I guess so."

His shoulders slumped slightly too, as if he were feeling some of her disappointment. "I mean, it might work in the short run, but what would happen when you wanted to get married for real?"

"Oh, I don't. I don't want to get married. All I've ever wanted to do is go to India and do this. It actually would work perfectly for me."

"Seriously? You don't want to get married?"

"It's not that I'm anti-marriage or anything. I've just never felt like I was called to be married. Some people aren't, you know."

"I know. I'm not married now either, of course. And if it weren't for Ellie, I'd be absolutely convinced my first marriage was a mistake."

There was that faint bitterness in his voice again, and this time it prompted a spark of hope. "Don't you want to get married again?"

"No." He met her eyes evenly.

"Why not?" It was too pushy, too intimate a question to ask a man she barely knew, but they were having this conversation and she needed to know. Some people found her forthrightness surprising, but it was the way she lived her life. She just didn't have patience to fiddle around with a lot of niceties.

"I don't know if I can trust a woman again. Enough to be married to her. For real, I mean."

She sucked in a sharp breath, the hope rising even more. "So, just to get it all on the table, we're talking about a marriage of convenience here, right?"

He turned his head away briefly. "This is crazy."

"I know it's crazy, but why shouldn't it work? If you have a wife, you could take on the codirector job. And if I had a husband who was called to missions work in India too, then everyone wouldn't balk at giving me money for support."

"You wouldn't even need to raise as much," he murmured. "They have an apartment in Bangalore for me."

"Wow," she breathed. "It's like it's meant to be."

"Let's not get ahead of ourselves though. Right now you might be sure that you don't want to get married for real, but what happens if that changes?"

"Why would you assume it's going to change?"

"How old are you?"

She straightened her spine. "Twenty-seven. What does that have to do with anything?"

"I'm thirty-eight. I've already been married and have a daughter. We're at different places in life. I'd feel like I was taking advantage of you."

She bit back a surge of anger and made herself say calmly, "That's condescending and a little offensive. I'm an adult. I'm not your eighteen-year-old babysitter anymore, and this is never going to work if you think about me as if I am. I know what I want. I'm capable of making mature, reasoned decisions. And this is the work I was put on this earth to do."

"I'm not trying to question your commitment or your certainty. But it feels like the perfect solution to my life just fell in my lap with you, and I don't want to be selfish and jump at the chance if it's not the right thing for you too."

"It *is* the right thing for me." She leaned forward and tried to convey her surety through her words and her expression. "It feels like the perfect solution to my life just fell in my lap too. There's a reason that Daniel wanted us to get together."

"I don't think he had a marriage of convenience in mind."

"Of course not. But there's a reason. Sometimes God works in inexplicable ways. Why not a marriage of convenience?"

His posture had relaxed, and he was almost smiling as he shook his head. "You know this is insane, right?"

"Of course it is. But think how perfect. We could work out all the details of how the marriage would work before-hand so things wouldn't be awkward. The only thing that's important to me is that we're faithful to each other. I don't believe in taking marriage casually."

"Me either," he said in a low voice. "I would be faithful."

She felt a strange sort of shiver at the words, but she didn't know where it was coming from, so she just ignored it. "Good. Me too. If we agree on that, then there's no reason we have to be in love to get married. We can set up the arrangement in a way that works for both of us. If you're not going to be in India all year round, then there will be a lot of time when we won't even be living on the same continent. That should make things easier. I really think it could work."

"You'd be okay with doing some sort of prenup? I need to think about Ellie and—"

"Of course. We'd get everything squared away so there are no surprises."

He was smiling now too and still looking faintly amused. "All right. If you're sure, then it definitely works for me."

"Great." She was suddenly so excited she wanted to hug herself. It was like her entire life was finally moving toward the end she'd been dreaming of. "Maybe I can actually get out there by next summer."

"That's when I'm hoping to go too."

She grinned at him. "See? It's like it's meant to be. Will your daughter be okay with it?"

"Why wouldn't she?"

"I don't know. It will just be a surprise that you're getting married."

"Ellie's a smart girl. She'll be fine."

"Okay. Good. Where are you living now anyway?"

"Raleigh. But I'll be moving to Willow Park eventually. You're back there, right?"

"Yeah. I'm just living with my parents as I raise support. I could always move to Raleigh for a while if that would make things easier."

"I'm selling the house in Raleigh anyway since it's way too big to keep up if I'm not in the States all year. I'll just move up the timeline and move to Willow Park over the next couple of months."

"Okay. Well, that would work well with me. It's a really nice town. Ellie will probably enjoy going to school there."

"Yeah. I hope so."

"Are you selling out your business then?"

"Not entirely. But I'm stepping way back in terms of my role so I can focus on the business center."

"It's a lot of big changes," she said, looking at the man across from her—handsome, successful, reserved—and wondering if it was possible that she was going to get married to him soon.

"I know. But good ones. Ellie is getting older, so I need to be there for her more, and there's no flexibility in the role I had in my business before. Besides, I just…"

"You just what?" It was another nosy question, but Lydia had never been reticent about asking what she wanted to know.

"I want to do something different."

She wondered what had happened with his ex-wife, but she wasn't quite comfortable enough with him to ask about it.

Even she had a few social boundaries.

"We should probably be engaged for a month or two, or no one will believe the relationship is real."

"Yeah," he said. "And that will give us some time to change our minds if we want to."

"Maybe we can get married before Christmas. That

would give us plenty of time to plan for getting to India over the summer.

"That sounds like a good timeline." He pulled out his phone and pulled up what was evidently a calendar. "I've got commitments through October, so I can try to sell the house by the end of next month. We should probably start dating now so the engagement doesn't come out of the blue and then announce the engagement at the first of November when Ellie and I move back to Willow Park. Then get married maybe December 6?"

Lydia pulled out her calendar and checked it too, feeling rather amused at planning out the schedule for their marriage of convenience. "Works for me. That gives us plenty of time to make sure we're able to get along and such. If you end up being a jerk, then I might have to back out."

He chuckled. "Same here."

"Good. I think this might actually work."

"All right then. I guess we have a deal." He gave her that half-amused, half-bitter smile and stretched out his hand across the table. "It's on then?"

She shook his hand, feeling a rush of excitement at how smoothly, easily, perfectly things had worked out.

This was definitely a gift from God.

She said, "This marriage is on."

CHAPTER 2

A MONTH LATER, LYDIA SAT ON A LEATHER LOVESEAT NEXT to Gabe and tried to look comfortable.

They were in Daniel's office in the church, and it was the first session of their premarital counseling since Daniel wouldn't marry couples who didn't go through at least three sessions of counseling first.

But talking about a marriage of convenience in front of her hometown pastor—whom she'd known all her life—wasn't exactly the most comfortable thing to do.

And there were still twenty minutes left to go.

She stared down at her hands, still finding it strange that there was an engagement ring on her left hand. It was simple—gold with a diamond solitaire—but it looked really expensive to Lydia. Much more expensive than anything she was used to wearing.

Gabe had given it to her a couple of weeks ago in a romantic gesture that consisted of thrusting the box at her and saying, "Here. You might wear this."

"Look," Daniel said, tugging at his brown hair the way

he did whenever he was thinking hard. "I'm not judging you or anything. Everyone has different reasons for getting married. Just be honest about what the reasons are."

Lydia glanced over at Gabe, trying to get a cue from him about how open they should be about this situation. They hadn't told Daniel why they were getting married, but he must have realized something was up.

For the past month they'd gotten together every weekend—since they were supposed to be dating. Twice she'd driven down to Raleigh, and twice Gabe had driven up to Willow Park. He didn't feel like a stranger to her anymore, and her first impression of his being a decent guy had been affirmed on every trip.

She understood the look in his eyes when he met her gaze, and she gave a little nod in response.

He cleared his throat. "Both Lydia and I are practical people. This marriage makes sense for us in every way we've considered—right now and for the future. We both really want it."

"We do," Lydia added just so it was clear Gabe wasn't putting words in her mouth. "I know it might seem a little strange to you—since you're so head-over-heels in love with Jessica—but we both really want it. We're committed to making it work."

A strange expression flickered across Daniel's face for just a few seconds before it returned to his characteristic thoughtful observation. "I had no idea what I was getting into when I married Jessica. And I love her so much more now than I did even a year ago. You know, the Bible tells us to love the person we're married to. It never tells us to marry the person we love. I don't look for desperate passion in couples since that's a pretty flimsy foundation for a lifelong commitment. I need to know that the couple is equally committed to their faith and the church, which I know you both are. And I need to know they're both entering the marriage with a clear understanding and a commitment to each other."

"We are," Lydia said, leaning forward, feeling better because Daniel hadn't thrown them out of his office in disgust when they'd admitted that the marriage was at least partly practical. "We're committed to this marriage. We're committed to each other."

Daniel shifted his eyes over to Gabe, who nodded.

"We're committed," he said.

"You can trust Lydia's commitment, despite what happened with Michaela?" Daniel asked him.

Michaela was Gabe's first wife. He hadn't told Lydia much about her, except she'd walked out on him five years ago and only sporadically wanted to see Ellie.

Gabe shifted in his seat just slightly. "Yes. They're two entirely different things."

It sounded like he meant it, and Lydia could basically understand why. He'd told her he couldn't trust another woman with his heart, but he wasn't asking for Lydia's heart.

He could trust Lydia's reasoned decision. Her heart wasn't relevant to him at all.

It made her feel strange—just a little pang of regret—but it faded almost immediately. This was better. Easier. Simpler. And it would finally get her to her calling in life.

"Why is it different?" Daniel asked.

"Michaela and I were infatuated kids. Lydia and I are adults who know what we're doing."

"Okay," Daniel said after a minute of watching Gabe closely. "I can't see any reason why you shouldn't get married. I'll be happy to marry you."

Lydia let out a breath, and she felt Gabe relax slightly too. They could easily have gone to the courthouse to get married or found another pastor to officiate, but they'd both been raised in this church. If they were going to get married, they wanted it to be here.

"So next time," Daniel said, glancing over a sheet of paper on his desk, "I need you both to write out expectations you have for the marriage."

"Expectations?" Lydia tried not to frown, but she hadn't been expecting homework.

"Yes," he said, his mouth twitching slightly as he looked at her. "Expectations. I have a list of things here for you to address."

"Okay," Lydia murmured, hoping it wasn't a very long list. Everything was going smoothly here. She was happier than she'd been in a year since it looked like her plans were finally coming to fruition.

But she didn't want to spend all kinds of time thinking about a marriage that was purely practical.

"You'll want to write these down," Daniel prompted.

Gabe pulled out his phone to take notes on, with a dry, slanted glance at Lydia as if he were questioning this too. And Lydia found an old receipt in her purse she could jot the list down on.

"Okay. So for next time, write out your expectations for the marriage regarding the following," Daniel said. "Work

—for both of you. Spiritual life. Money. Raising Ellie. Household duties. Handling disagreements. Sex."

Lydia jerked in surprise. Unfortunately, she was pretty sure that Gabe could feel it. She was okay with writing down how she thought they should divvy up household chores, but she was not too happy about writing out her expectations for sex.

Her expectations were that they weren't going to have sex.

"Write it down," Daniel prompted, evidently noticing that she'd paused. "There's more. Recreation—and by that I mean things like date nights and family time and vacations."

Lydia kept writing out the list as Daniel continued, but she was intensely aware of Gabe sitting beside her.

In a matter of weeks, the man was going to be her husband.

It was a very strange kind of thing to process.

Gabe's parents had been watching Ellie as she played on the church playground equipment during their counseling session, and from there Gabe and Lydia were going to take her to the new house.

Gabe paused, however, in the hallway of the church after they left Daniel's office. "So what did you think?" he asked, studying her face closely.

She shrugged, trying to look casual since she didn't want him to think that she was flustered by some of what had been discussed. "It was fine. I think it went fine."

"Good."

He wasn't much of a talker. She was learning that about him. She figured it was a good thing since guys who had to be the center of attention all the time drove her crazy.

"I didn't realize we were going to have homework though," she added, keeping her voice down so Daniel wouldn't hear.

"Yeah." Gabe started walking again, putting a casual hand on her back to get her to fall in step with him. "We should go through our answers before next week so we're on the same page about all that."

"I think we were supposed to write the answers out separately so we can see where our expectations differ."

"I know. But I'm not about to talk through differing expectations about money and sex when Daniel is in the room."

"Oh." She swallowed hard, feeling her face grow a little hot at the idea. She was a normal woman and had all the normal biological urges for sex, but she'd intentionally not focused on them. For a long time she'd been so determined to pursue her plans for the future that she just hadn't had time to worry about it. In addition, she'd worked with enough women who'd been sexually abused that she was under no romantic delusions about sex.

Under the right circumstances, sex was very likely a nice thing to do, but it wasn't as important—or as fulfilling —as making a difference in the world.

"Good point. Although some of that should be pretty easy. Right?" She lowered her voice to a hush, so much so that he had to step forward—very close to her—to hear. "I mean, we aren't going to have sex, are we?"

"Not if you don't want to." He'd ducked his head slightly, still looking her in the eye.

She was suddenly breathless—overly warm and overly conscious of his big body in front of her. "You weren't expecting to, were you? I mean, this is purely practical, isn't it?"

"It is. I'd be perfectly willing to make sex part of the arrangement, but it's not a deal breaker either way."

She swallowed hard and closed her fingers since they were shaking slightly. "You were thinking we might have sex?"

He seemed very quiet and intense at the moment, so she was surprised when a little smile quirked on the corner of his lips. "I didn't know what you were expecting. As I said, I'm fine either way. You didn't think I'd say no if you were going to offer sex, did you?"

Torn between embarrassment and amusement, Lydia lowered her eyes. "I hadn't thought about it. Sex would complicate things, wouldn't it?"

"Why would it?"

She looked back up and was suddenly imagining those sexy, blue, heavy-lidded eyes looking at her from the pillow beside her. Her whole body tightened, and she had to look away. "I don't know. It just seems like sex has the potential to make things kind of… messy. I think it would be easier and simpler if we just don't."

"Okay. That's fine with me. But you can change your mind anytime you want. It's a standing offer."

She gulped and took a breath, telling herself she was a grown woman who had a lot more important things going on than turning into a puddle of goo over the idea of sex with her husband of convenience.

"Okay," she said. She suddenly realized that, at some point, she must have raised one of her hands to put on his chest. It was pressed against his shirt, just over his heart. He felt real, solid, beneath her palm.

She pulled it away quickly. "Okay. We'll say no to sex for now, leaving open the possibility of that changing. It's probably a good idea to go over the other stuff so the discussion doesn't get awkward at the next session. Good thinking."

"I do think well occasionally," he murmured, slanting her another amused look.

For such a reserved man, he had a really good sense of humor.

She liked that about him.

She was hiding a smile when they walked out the back door to the fenced-off part of the grounds that held the playground equipment.

Ellie wasn't playing on the playground. She was reading a book on a bench while her grandparents sat on another bench.

Lydia didn't feel like she'd gotten to know the girl very well since Ellie was evidently as quiet as her dad. But she'd always been perfectly polite whenever Lydia had spent time with her and Gabe, so Lydia assumed the girl would warm up as time went on.

After all, if Gabe and Ellie were going to be in the States during the school year, then it wasn't like Lydia would be around her full time.

When Ellie glanced up and saw her father, she jumped

up and ran over to him, her dark hair flying out behind her.

She grabbed Gabe in a hug, which he returned as if they'd been parted for days rather than less than an hour.

"Were you reading the whole time," he asked, stroking the girl's long hair.

"No." She pulled away and stared up at her father soberly. "I talked to Grandma and Grandpa some."

"Good. Are you ready to go check out our new house?" he asked.

"Yes." Ellie was darting looks up at Lydia as she talked, but she didn't smile.

Lydia smiled at her, thinking it was sweet that the girl and Gabe were so close. It made sense since her mother had abandoned her so early.

"Everything okay?" Gabe asked, turning to his parents, who had gotten up from the bench and were approaching more slowly.

"Oh yes," his mother said, smiling kindly at both of them. "How did the session go?"

"It was—" Gabe broke off when his phone rang. After he glanced at it, he said, "I'm sorry. I better take this."

He walked over to the other side of the yard as he picked up.

Lydia assumed it was business. He often got business calls when they spent time together. She didn't care. He could work as much as he wanted for all she cared.

She was planning to spend most of her time working too—once she finally got to India.

"Those business calls," his mother said, tsking her tongue and then smiling at Lydia. "You'll have your work cut out, trying to get him to turn the phone off sometimes."

Lydia smiled back, feeling a little awkward since Gabe's parents obviously believed theirs was a normal marriage. "I'll do my best."

"I'm so happy he found someone," Mary Alexander went on, looking back toward her son. "We were so surprised. But so happy. After what happened—"

"Mary," Henry, her husband, murmured in a mild, soft tone. It sounded like a reminder to not say more than was appropriate.

"Right," Mary said, looking apologetic. "Anyway, all I meant to say is that we're so happy Gabe will have a wife and Ellie will finally have a mama." She patted the girl's shoulder. "Aren't you happy, sweetheart?"

"Yes." Ellie still wasn't smiling. Just gazing between her grandmother and Lydia with unchildlike sobriety.

"Sorry," Gabe said, returning to where they were standing. "I need to get pulled into a conference call for twenty minutes or so. Would you mind taking Ellie to Jean's to get a donut while I'm on the phone? Then I could meet you at the house."

"Sure," Lydia said, wondering what she was going to do with this quiet girl for a half hour on her own. "That's no problem. Do you want to go with me for a donut, Ellie?"

Ellie opened her mouth but closed it again as she looked up at her father's face. He was giving her a little nod. Then she said, "Okay."

"Good."

Lydia didn't dislike children. She'd always thought they were fine but not really her thing. She'd certainly never spent much time around them other than occasional babysitting as a teenager.

But she was determined to do her duty as Gabe's wife, no matter what it entailed since she was getting so much out of the arrangement. So she put on a calm, friendly demeanor as she thanked and said good-bye to Gabe's parents and then walked to the parking lot, where Ellie got into Lydia's car.

"Thanks," Gabe said quietly after he'd shut the door for his daughter. "You don't mind, do you?"

"No, it's fine," Lydia told him with a smile.

"I won't be long." He looked over the roof of her car to where his parents were getting into their van. "They're watching," he said in a low voice.

She had no idea why he'd said that or why it mattered, so she was completely taken by surprise when he leaned forward and kissed her gently on the lips.

It was just a brief kiss. Light. Not much of anything at all.

But Lydia felt a rush of shocked excitement and couldn't speak or move for a moment afterward.

One part of her mind understood that his parents were observing them, so Gabe was trying to act like a fiancé would.

But all the rest of her mind and body were screaming that he'd kissed her.

"Is that okay?" he asked, evidently seeing something in her expression. "They think we're in love, and I don't want to disappoint them again."

She pushed through her reaction to say in a somewhat natural tone. "Sure. Of course. No problem."

She was still feeling rather rattled, though, as she got into the driver's seat and started her car. "You ready for a donut?"

Ellie eyed her somberly. "Okay."

There wasn't anything obvious to say next, so Lydia was quiet as she pulled the car out of the lot and headed for the little bakery/coffee shop on Willow Park's quaint downtown street.

She wondered, a little distractedly, how Gabe had disappointed his parents before.

Realizing that Ellie was still staring at her, Lydia said cheerfully, "So what kind of donut are you going to get?"

"Chocolate frosting."

"Oh, that sounds good."

She waited, but Ellie didn't have anything else to say. She still wasn't smiling.

How the hell was she supposed to know what to say to get the girl to relax and warm up? She felt kind of clueless, and she clearly wasn't getting any miraculous insight at the moment.

She'd spent time with Ellie before but only in Gabe's company, so they'd never had a real conversation of their own.

Ellie didn't seem to even like her.

Lydia was searching her mind for something light and fun to say when Ellie asked without prelude, "Why did Dad kiss you?"

Lydia felt just as much at a loss for words as she had by the car when Gabe had kissed her. She had no idea what she was supposed to say to such a question. "Well, uh, your dad and I are going to get married. He told you about that, didn't he?"

"Yes." The deep blue eyes were unnaturally cool for a child. "He told me. I didn't know he was going to kiss you."

Lydia flushed slightly, feeling ridiculously embarrassed —which was an absolutely unreasonable reaction to a conversation with a girl. "He might sometimes," she said at last, continuing to glance over to check Ellie's expression.

"Oh." The girl paused as if she were thinking something through. "I don't really want another mom."

Oh, this was a terrible conversation. How could she possibly get out of it?

Lydia was used to being efficient and no-nonsense with everyone she encountered, but she spoke slowly, as gently as she could. "Well, I'm going to be your dad's wife, but that doesn't mean I'll be your mom."

"My mom left when I was really little."

Lydia's hands clenched on the steering wheel. "I know she did."

"Why do you have to be his wife?"

"Well, we both want to be married. I know it's a big change for you, but I think it's going to be good for all of us."

"Daddy and I are fine by ourselves."

Shit. Clearly, Ellie wasn't at all happy about the upcoming marriage, and Lydia had no idea how to change her mind.

She wasn't any good with kids at all.

"I'm sure you were fine, but maybe you can be even better. I promise I'll never try to take him away from you."

They'd reached Main Street, so Lydia slowed down to look for a parking space.

Ellie was silent until Lydia pulled the car into a space not far from Jean's.

Then the girl said, "He loves me best."

Lydia was so uncomfortable with this conversation and so confused about what she should say that she felt like jumping out of the car and running away. But she turned to look Ellie in the eyes since she realized the girl was taking this very seriously.

She had no idea what to say, and she had no idea what would make things worse. So the only thing to say was what she always tried to say. The truth.

"Yes," she said, "your dad loves you best."

The conversation over donuts was just as stilted and awkward as it had been in the car, but at least eating the donuts created natural pauses in conversation.

Ellie clearly hadn't warmed up to her at all when they drove over to the house Gabe had bought.

The price of real estate was higher in Willow Park than in the surrounding areas because the town was a popular magnet for travelers looking for quaint, small-town charm, beautiful mountain scenery, and regional crafts and antiques. But most of the houses in town were older and between two and four bedrooms.

The house Gabe had bought was on one of the more prestigious streets with a huge yard and six bedrooms. For

Gabe, though, it was downsizing. The house he'd owned in Charlotte was even bigger and more expensive.

He'd bought this house straight-out. Hadn't even needed a mortgage.

Lydia didn't know the extent of his financial worth, but he was definitely richer than anyone else she knew.

She didn't really care about it one way or the other. She'd never been particularly concerned with material things. All of this was transitory anyway since she was going to live in India.

Gabe must have just pulled in a minute before them since he was getting out of the car as she parked.

He was still talking on the phone, but he hung up a few seconds after he saw them.

"How was the donut?" he asked as Ellie scrambled out of the car and ran over to him.

"Fine. I had chocolate frosting."

"We got you one too," Lydia said, walking over to them with the takeout bag. "Ellie said you liked blueberry."

"I do. Thank you." He looked into the bag.

"Aren't you going to eat it?" Ellie asked.

"Of course." Put on the spot, he pulled out the donut and took a bite. "Let's go check out the house."

Neither Ellie nor Lydia had been inside the house before, so he gave them the tour.

It was built in the twenties, but it had been beautifully restored and renovated, and even Lydia—who never suffered from house envy much—gawked at each lovely, spacious room.

Gabe had invited her to help with the house hunting, but she'd only gone on a few token visits. It was going to be his house, after all. She would hardly be living in it after this winter and spring. She didn't really need to weigh in.

Ellie had gone through the rooms on the ground floor more quickly than the adults and was already running up the stairs.

"Be careful," Gabe called. "If you fall down, you'll have to just lie there until we catch up."

"I never fall down."

He smiled and shook his head as they walked into the kitchen—stainless steel appliances, beautiful cherry cabinets that were done to reflect the period of the house, and a very cool-looking countertop on the center island.

"What is this?" she asked, running her hand across it.

"It's quartz." Gabe was dressed casually in a blue shirt and tan trousers, and he seemed to fill the room more than he should. "Micah Duncan flipped this house a few years ago, and the couple he sold it to had to move out of the area."

Micah was Daniel's brother, and she'd grown up with him. "Micah did? No wonder it looks so great."

"He knows what he's doing." Gabe glanced over at her. "I guess he's around your age."

"Yeah. We dated in high school, actually." She smiled since she'd always liked Micah, and she'd been thrilled when he finally settled down and married the girl he'd been in love with for years.

"Did you?"

There was an odd timbre to the tone, so Lydia glanced over at him. She couldn't read anything in his expression though. "Yeah. He's a really great guy."

Gabe glanced away. "Well, he does great work. The

house is in excellent shape. Do you want to see the upstairs?"

"Sure."

They were heading up the stairs when Ellie came running down.

"Can I have the room in the attic?" she asked, gazing up at her dad.

He reached out to steady her since she'd stopped so abruptly she wobbled a bit. "Of course. You can have any room you want." He looked back at Lydia and explained, "There's a little garret room on the third floor. It's not really the attic."

Lydia didn't care if it was the attic or not. And she didn't care that he'd given Ellie her pick of rooms in the house without even asking her first.

What she was thinking was that it was a good thing she had no expectations of feelings to come along with this marriage.

Because she could easily read the look in Gabe's eyes as he looked down at his daughter.

And it was more than obvious that Ellie had been right in what she'd said earlier.

There was no way any woman could have an equal place in his heart.

CHAPTER 3

"IF YOU NEED HELP," GABE SAID, STANDING AT THE DOOR TO the dressing room in a department store, "just open the door."

"I don't need help," Ellie said from the other side.

Lydia was in the dressing room too, standing a little farther back from Gabe. She could see from the opening beneath the door that Ellie had put on the long dress with a thick lace hem they'd picked out, but the fabric kept moving so the girl was clearly still working on the buttons.

"It's hard to get all the buttons if they're in the back," Lydia said, trying to sound light and friendly, although she was tired and a little bored since the shopping trip to buy Ellie a dress for the wedding was taking longer than she'd expected.

The girl was nine, but she clearly had very concrete ideas about the dress she wanted.

It wasn't surprising that she was a little spoiled since it had just been Gabe and Ellie for years. Lydia tried to remind herself of this fact and remain patient even as the girl rejected dress after adorable dress—all of which looked equally nice on her.

"I can do the buttons myself," Ellie said from behind the door.

"Okay." Gabe turned and gave Lydia a half smile. "Take your time."

He stepped over to Lydia and leaned against the wall beside her. "I think we're almost done here," he said, very low. "She seemed to like this one the best."

Lydia nodded, realizing that he must have recognized her impatience. "No problem. We're not in a hurry."

He raised his eyebrows with a warm irony that made her smile.

"Patience isn't my virtue," she admitted softly since he'd obviously sensed her mood. "But it's really fine. She should get the dress she really likes, especially since this is going to be a big transition for her."

"She'll do fine."

Gabe didn't seem worried as she studied his face, noticing—and not for the first time—how strong and masculine the square jaw, the slight stubble, the well-chiseled cheekbones were. There was a very faint scattering of gray in his dark hair.

He felt solid. She liked that about him.

It was more than evident that Ellie had hidden her displeasure about this marriage from him, and Lydia felt uncomfortable saying anything since it felt like she was either tattling or complaining.

Ellie hadn't done anything that was genuinely naughty. She'd just made it clear that she wished Lydia wasn't around.

"I got all the buttons but two," Ellie said, opening the dressing room door.

She looked very pretty in the feminine dress, but it didn't appear to be hanging right.

"Maybe Miss Lydia can get the last two buttons for you," Gabe said, straightening up.

Ellie frowned. "I thought she was Aunt Lydia now."

"Oh. That's right. You can call her whichever you'd like."

They'd had a long conversation about what Ellie should call Lydia. It would feel wrong to Lydia for Ellie to call her some version of "mom," so she'd said she'd rather they not suggest that to Ellie. Gabe flatly refused to let the girl call her just "Lydia," which would have been Lydia's preference since he didn't allow his daughter to call adults by just their first names. So they'd compromised on Aunt Lydia, which was frankly a little weird but was the best they could come up with.

There were all kinds of strange details to work out when planning for a marriage of convenience.

Ellie was still frowning. "I want *you* to do the buttons."

"But my fingers are too big to mess with little buttons like that." Gabe caught the girl's eye in an expression Lydia was starting to recognize—the silent reminder that she needed to be good.

"Okay," Ellie said with a frown, turning around in front of Lydia.

Lydia saw what was wrong with the hang of the dress as the girl showed her the back. She'd misbuttoned a couple of the buttons, so the fabric wasn't aligned straight.

Lydia squatted down and gently undid two of the

buttons and redid them.

"What are you doing?" Ellie asked, looking back over her shoulder. "Those weren't the ones."

Lydia wasn't about to tell the girl she'd buttoned the dress wrong. With a smile, she replied, "I like these little pearl buttons so much I was checking them out. Here you go—you're all buttoned now."

Ellie peered at Lydia suspiciously, but then she got distracted by the dress.

"It's beautiful," Lydia said, praying that this was the last dress they needed to try on. She'd never been big on shopping—even for herself.

Ellie peered at herself in the big mirror, turning around and inspecting the dress from every angle.

"I really like it," Gabe said. "I think that's the one." He hadn't shown any of the impatience that Lydia felt, but she was sure that shopping wasn't at the top of his list of things to do either.

Ellie didn't say anything for a long time. Then she finally turned around and faced her father. "This one is it."

Lydia almost slumped with relief, and she felt Gabe relax too. "Excellent," he said. "Let Aunt Lydia unbutton it for you, and then you can change clothes so we can go get something for lunch."

Lydia didn't like being "Aunt Lydia." She also didn't like being "Miss Lydia." And it would definitely be wrong for her to be called "Mom."

Whatever she was to Ellie clearly didn't have any sort of name.

Pushing the thought aside, she unbuttoned the dress quickly and stared at the bottom of the dressing room door as Ellie changed clothes, recognizing every step of the process by the inches she could see beneath the door.

When she glanced over, she saw that Gabe was watching her.

She had no idea what to make of his expression, so she just smiled.

He smiled back, but it didn't reach his eyes. She wondered what he'd been thinking about and if he was, for some reason, unhappy with her.

She didn't want him to be unhappy. This marriage was the way to finally get what she wanted. She needed to make sure she didn't look impatient again.

"We can add a red satin sash to the dress for the wedding," Lydia said brightly when Ellie emerged dressed in her sweater and blue corduroy pants. "That's what Mia is going to wear with her dress."

Mia was Lydia's five-year-old niece—her brother's daughter.

"I like pink better."

Shit. Even her attempts to be friendly always seemed to backfire. "I like pink too, but since it's Christmas, all the flowers are going to be red. So a red sash would match better."

"Oh."

"You can have pink if you—" Lydia began. The wedding was going to be very small. No one but family. If it meant the girl would be happy, Lydia didn't care if her dress didn't match.

But Gabe interrupted, "You like red too, don't you, Ellie?"

"Yes. I guess so. But I wanted a pink sash."

"A pink sash won't match the flowers. So you can have a red sash or you can have no sash. Whichever you'd like." His voice was a little sterner than normal. Not much, but it obviously had an impact on Ellie.

The girl's head dropped. "I'll have a red sash," she mumbled.

"All right then."

"It will be really pretty," Lydia said, feeling bad that she'd somehow gotten the girl in trouble with her dad and not wanting Ellie to blame her for it. "We can make it hang down really long like the dress. We can do a knot or a big bow in the back."

Ellie looked up at her soberly. "Bows are for little girls."

"Okay. Then Mia can have the bow and you can let your sash hang down. There are wedding dresses that are made like that sometimes. And your flowers will be red tulips that match."

"I like tulips." The girl wasn't smiling, but she looked a little less upset.

Feeling encouraged by this progress, Lydia said, "I do too. They're my favorite flowers."

As they stood waiting to pay, Gabe stroked Ellie's hair. She leaned against him, and he put his arm around her.

Lydia felt an odd, completely irrational pang in her chest.

They were clearly family—as close as people could get. She wasn't part of it. She might be marrying Gabe, but she wasn't going to be part of this family. She would always be an outsider.

Someone without even a good name to be called.

It was fine. It was what she wanted. She couldn't have

ties like this if she wanted to devote herself to her work in India. It would only pull her away from her calling.

This was all part of the transitory life she would be leaving behind.

But still her chest ached a little as they left the store.

They ate lunch at a restaurant in the mall that had macaroni and cheese that Ellie liked, and they were on their way out when Lydia saw familiar faces.

"Micah," she called, seeing the couple walking with a toddler beyond the sunglasses stand. "Alice."

Daniel's brother, Micah, turned and grinned when he saw her. He was an attractive, rugged man with a warm smile, and his wife Alice was quiet and sweet with beautiful, long, wavy hair that Lydia had always envied.

Lydia liked both of them, so she was smiling for real as they approached with their daughter, Cara.

Lydia gave Micah and then Alice a big hug, feeling more comfortable than she had before—since these were people she really knew and understood.

Gabe and Ellie she didn't really know. And she didn't really understand them.

"We heard the news," Micah said, looking almost rakish as he grinned at her. "Congratulations."

"Thanks." Lydia was a little embarrassed, the way she always was when she introduced Gabe as her fiancé, but she managed to hide it. "This is Gabe. And this is his daughter, Ellie."

Micah and Gabe shook hands, and then Alice, who was

chasing after Cara, waved and said it was nice to meet him.

"Have we met before?" Micah asked, giving Gabe a close look.

"I don't think so."

"You know Mary and Henry from church, right? He's their son. But he's a lot older than us, so he was in college by the time we were in school."

She glanced up at Gabe and saw he'd tightened his lips, and she realized that maybe she shouldn't have said he was old.

She was terrible at being a fiancée.

She stepped over toward him and tried to think of something nice to say to temper the "old" comment, but she couldn't think of anything. "But he bought one of your houses," she added to Micah. "The one on Elm."

"I love that house," Micah said, still smiling and watching them with a slightly questioning expression.

Gabe reached out to put an arm around Lydia, pulling her against his side with a gesture that must look affectionate. "We love it too. You did a really good job with it."

Alice had returned with Cara in tow. "So when is the wedding?" she asked, holding Cara with one hand and pulling a stray thread from Micah's shirt with the other.

"December 6," Lydia said, feeling kind of strange in Gabe's embrace but being sure not to pull away. "It's just family though. We don't want any big hoopla."

"Maybe we can do a dinner or something for you all afterward then," Alice said. "We want to celebrate with you in some way. I'll talk to Jessica about it. If you don't mind, of course."

"I'm sure that will be fine," Lydia replied since she

couldn't figure out any good way to refuse. They were keeping things low-key on purpose since it felt like a lie to go through all the normal wedding traditions in their situation. "Thank you for thinking about it."

"Of course. I'm so excited for you."

Lydia understood that Alice was being genuine and that she was also surprised. It wasn't all that long ago that she'd told Alice straight-out that she didn't think she would ever get married.

She hated people to think she was wrong like that.

"We better get going," Gabe said, glancing over at Ellie, who had been watching the proceedings with typical silence. "It was good to meet you both."

After they said farewells, they continued walking toward the exit. Ellie walked a few feet ahead, and Gabe kept his hand on the small of Lydia's back.

He gave her a strange look but didn't say anything.

"What is it?" she asked since she figured it was better to keep things open between them.

"Since we're supposed to be engaged, it might be a good idea for you to act as though you like me as much as you like other people."

Lydia stiffened slightly, feeling immediately defensive at what was clearly a reproach, however mild and casual his tone.

"What did I do?" She'd called him "old," but it didn't sound like that was what he was referring to.

"You appeared happier to see Micah than you were to be with me." He wasn't looking at her. He was watching Ellie walk in front of them.

"Oh." Lydia thought about that, realizing he was right.

She had been happy to see Micah and Alice since they were friends, familiar, comfortable. Nothing at all like Gabe.

"Especially since you used to be with Micah."

Lydia sucked in a surprised breath and looked up to scan Gabe's face. He'd sounded almost jealous.

But he definitely had a point about her needing to treat him more like a future husband. "Sorry," she said. "This is new. And strange."

"I know." His face, when she checked, looked natural again. He never revealed very much, but he didn't appear to be unhappy with her anymore.

"I'll do better."

She felt guilty and rattled as they walked through the parking lot, but she comforted herself with the thought that this in-between time wouldn't last very long.

Soon she'd leave it all behind her. Soon she'd be who she wanted to be.

Two weekends later, just after Thanksgiving, Gabe and Lydia were moving her stuff into the house.

She'd been living with her parents since she graduated from law school, so she didn't actually have all that much stuff. She had her clothes and her incidentals, plus a few pieces of furniture.

Gabe had professional movers move him from Raleigh, but they were doing Lydia's stuff on their own.

Ellie was with her grandparents for the day, which was a good thing. Even given the minimal amount of Lydia's belongings, neither she nor Gabe were in very good moods as they carried her favorite chair upstairs into the bedroom that would be hers in the house.

"Damn it," Gabe muttered. "You need to keep walking."

"I'm trying." She felt like she was holding the whole weight of the chair although she knew it wasn't true. "Slow down a little."

He was in front, and she was behind, and unfortunately the stairs were old and rather steep.

"Do you have it?" he asked, shifting somehow in a way that took some of the weight of the chair off Lydia.

"I have it." She mostly had it although the chair was so wide that she couldn't get a good grip on it.

"Do you have it?" he asked again as he started ascending the stairs.

"I have it!"

The man really was the bossiest, most frustrating man in the world.

"Do you have it?" he asked again as they neared the top of the stairs.

Lydia's arms were shaking, and she could barely see through the perspiration. He was moving fast now, and she couldn't keep up.

"Wait!" she cried when she felt the chair slipping from her arms. "I don't have it."

He made a growling sound as he stopped, crouching down to keep hold of the chair as it lowered quickly to the stairs after it slipped from Lydia's grip.

"I'm sorry," she said, keeping the chair from falling down the stairs with her body. She panted and tried to summon her energy and coordination again. "You were moving too fast."

He gave her a narrow-eyed look over the chair. "You said you had it."

"I had it until you moved too fast."

He took a few deep breaths, his expression changing as he looked at her. "Are you okay?"

She straightened up, realizing he thought she was too feeble to carry the chair. "I'm fine. I'm ready. Let's get going again."

So they hefted the chair back up and managed to get it into the corner of her room where she wanted it.

They'd agreed they wouldn't be sharing a bedroom. They shouldn't have very many visitors up on the second floor of the house, and if someone noticed, they could find an excuse.

Lydia was fully prepared to announce to one and all that Gabe snored like a freight train.

When they got the chair in place, Lydia collapsed on the bare mattress of her bed, feeling like she'd been through a war.

"I told you I could have had the movers get your stuff."

"I know. But it wasn't all packed last week, and I don't have that much stuff. The chair was the worst."

Gabe was wearing jeans and a T-shirt, and as she watched, he lifted the bottom of his T-shirt to wipe the sweat off his face. She couldn't help but catch a glimpse of his flat belly before he let the shirt drop again.

He really had a very good body. Very good shoulders. Very good abs. Very good arms.

Lydia got up from the bed quickly and told herself to get a grip.

Her back caught, and she winced slightly.

"Are you okay?" he asked a little gruffly as she leaned over to stretch out her back.

"Yeah. I'm fine. I'm not going to fall apart from carrying a chair upstairs, you know. I'm in pretty good shape."

She wasn't built like a model, but she was tall with long limbs, and she liked to run and swim.

"I know you're in good shape."

His voice sounded strange again, so she glanced over at him as she straightened up. He was eyeing her body.

She was suddenly conscious of both her body and his. She'd been wearing an oversized hoodie earlier, but she'd taken it off when she'd gotten hot, so now she just had on a pair of leggings and a T-shirt that wasn't quite long enough.

She recognized something in his expression, in his tense stance, that gave her a shiver of excitement.

He'd told her that sex was a standing offer, and she was suddenly picturing what it might be like for him to take her to bed.

She'd never had sex before since she'd always been committed to waiting until marriage. In the past year or so, she'd been starting to wonder if she'd remain a virgin all her life. She hadn't thought that would be all that bad.

She wasn't sure why, ever since she'd met Gabe, she'd started thinking so much about sex.

After a minute, she turned away from him abruptly, worried that he might recognize what she was thinking.

This marriage wasn't for her to indulge in sex. It was for her to get over to India.

That was what was most important. These unexpected feelings for Gabe definitely weren't.

CHAPTER 4

LYDIA STARED AT HERSELF IN THE MIRROR, WONDERING IF the reflection was really her in the wedding dress.

She had a fairly large circle of friends, so she'd been part of a lot of weddings, and she'd seen many brides who —in an effort to look as beautiful as possible on their wedding day—ended up with hair, makeup, and dress that made them look like an entirely different person.

Maybe that was the point, but she'd always secretly thought some of them would have looked better and prettier if they'd toned it down and looked more like themselves.

Her hair was hanging down around her shoulders, and she didn't have on a lot of makeup. If it hadn't been for the dress, she could have been ready to start any other day.

Instead, she was getting married in an hour.

"Are you sure you don't want to do something else with your hair?" asked Martha Hendricks, the wife of one the church elders and self-appointed wedding organizer.

Lydia liked the woman just fine—despite her busybody

qualities—but she wouldn't have invited her to the wedding if her mother hadn't insisted.

"It's good this way. I don't like it to look too fancy or unnatural." Her hair glowed red and was hanging in a shiny fall to her shoulders. "I don't want a big fuss."

"You look beautiful," her mother said, coming over to stand near her and inspecting Lydia in the mirror. "I'm so glad you chose that dress."

Lydia would have chosen a much simpler dress, but her mother was so excited about the wedding and Lydia didn't like to disappoint her. The dress she'd ended up with had wide straps, a fitted waist, and a full skirt—with ruffles on the neckline and big flounces down the skirt. It wasn't too over the top, but Lydia still felt a little strange in it.

"Maybe a little more lipstick, dear," Martha said, coming toward her with the tube.

Lydia jerked away slightly and had to bite her lip to keep from saying something rude to the older woman, whom she'd known all her life.

"Martha," Lydia's mother said, "maybe you could go out and check on Ellie and Mia—to make sure they're ready to go."

This suggestion pleased everyone since it gave Martha a way to be helpful and also got her out of the room.

"You don't need any more lipstick," her mother said with a smile when Martha had left. "You look beautiful."

"Well, I look like myself, and I guess that's all I can expect." Lydia smiled to make sure her mom knew the self-deprecation was teasing.

"Of course it is. And it's all that Gabe will want."

Lydia didn't have a response to that comment.

"I can't believe you're not even nervous," her mom said.

"Why would I be nervous?"

"Most women are for one reason or another. But you're as cool as a cucumber, as always."

Lydia wondered, if she'd been marrying a man she loved, whether she'd be all fluttery and jittery like most of the brides she'd known. She couldn't even imagine. As it was, she mostly wanted to get this day over with—get these next few months over with—so she could get over to India and get started. "This is what I want, so I'm not sure why I'd be nervous about it."

Her mother was about to say something when Lydia's phone chirped with a text. She glanced over at her purse in surprise—somehow not expecting to get any messages on her wedding day—but she walked over to pull the phone out to check.

It was Gabe, who was just in another room of the church. *Everything good?*

She raised her eyebrows as she tapped out her response. *Of course. Why wouldn't it be?*

Just checking. No second thoughts?

Not from me. What about you?

Not from me either.

This is what I want.

Me too.

Good.

Okay. See you out there.

Despite herself, she almost giggled at his last text. It was nice that he was double-checking. He was a really nice guy.

"That must be from Gabe," her mom said. "I'd recognize that expression anywhere."

Lydia dropped her eyes and felt her cheeks redden.

"No need to be embarrassed," her mom said with another smile.

She hadn't been embarrassed about being caught with soft feelings, but because her mom had so drastically misunderstood. She shook off the reaction though since it didn't really matter.

"You're not nervous about... about tonight, are you?" Her mom looked a little self-conscious as she fussed with Lydia's skirt.

Lydia hid a smile. Her mother didn't like to talk about sex, but she was clearly making an effort now in case her daughter needed it. "I'm twenty-seven, Mom. I'm pretty sure I know how things work."

"I know. I was just making sure. I just hope that you... It's easy to expect too much and then to be disappointed, and I don't want that to happen with you."

Lydia was surprised by this stilted admission, and she turned to meet her mom's eyes. "Why would I be disappointed? Gabe is..." She trailed off, not sure what exactly Gabe was.

"Oh, I'm sure Gabe is wonderful. That's not the point. It's that girls now seem to have all these overinflated views of what sex is—fed by books and stories and all that—like it's going to transport them to some alternate reality. And then when it gets down to it, it's still just you. And him. And sometimes it's good, and sometimes it's something you do because you love the other person, and occasionally it blows you away, but you're always going to be just you, and he's always going to be just him. In bed and out of it."

The words rang true to Lydia—and she knew they were

hard for her mother to say—so she didn't brush them aside or laugh them off. Her mother didn't know that she wasn't planning to have sex with Gabe, and she was being a good mother—as she'd always been. "Thanks, Mom."

Her mother gave her a one-armed hug that wouldn't wrinkle her dress. "I'm so happy for you, dear. I used to worry... but I'm so happy for you."

Lydia returned the hug, but when she pulled away, she asked, "What did you worry about?"

"Nothing big. You were always so together, and you always knew what you wanted. That's a good thing. I'm so proud of you." Her mother cleared her throat before she continued, "I see a lot of girls living their lives like they're in a holding pattern before marriage. Like only when they find their man will they truly begin to live. You were never like that. But sometimes I wondered if, instead of marriage, you were doing the same thing with your work in India. It's a good thing. It's such a good thing. But I wondered if you were just putting life on hold before you got there. But I was wrong. You're obviously not. And now you're going to have a husband and a stepdaughter, and I'm so happy for you."

Her mother hugged her again, obviously overwhelmed with feeling, and Lydia hugged back. Because she was her mother. And because she loved her.

But she really wanted to pull away.

The marriage was going to be real—based on love or not—but it suddenly felt like there was something about it that was a lie.

~

Lydia hadn't been nervous about the wedding at all—not once. And she wasn't nervous when she left the Sunday school room that was acting as the dressing room and went to stand in the narthex.

There were only thirty-two people attending the wedding, but she was still going to process, with Ellie and Mia as the flower girls so her mother wouldn't be disappointed.

Lydia had two older brothers who had already gotten married—although Thomas was now separated from his wife. He approached her now, holding Mia's hand.

He gave her a smile. "You don't look too bad."

Thomas had always been super-smart and super-ambitious. After years of medical school and residencies, they'd all expected him to take some hotshot position as a surgeon at a major hospital. Instead, he'd moved back to the area last year so he could be closer to Mia, and he worked at the local hospital.

He was six years older than her, and they were closer now than they'd been growing up.

"You don't look too bad either," she told him. "And, Mia, you look beautiful."

"Thank you." Mia pushed her little glasses up her nose and held her long dress out for all to admire.

"You sure about this?" Thomas asked softly.

Lydia wasn't sure if he suspected something was atypical with her marriage or not, but she told him the truth either way. "Yes. I'm sure."

She was sure but was also starting to feel a little shaky as Martha fussed with her dress and she heard the music changing in the sanctuary.

It was so strange—because she was never shaky like that.

The feeling had come out of nowhere, but Lydia was suddenly chilly with something akin to nerves.

"Are you excited, Ellie?" she asked, trying to distract herself when she realized her hands were actually trembling as she held her bouquet.

Ellie looked adorable in her white dress and red satin sash tied in a decorative knot at the back. But she wasn't smiling as she waited silently for her time to process. "I know how to hold my flowers," she said.

That wasn't what she'd asked her, but Lydia didn't object. Her ears were starting to roar as she heard the wedding anthem begin. "You'll hold them perfectly, I'm sure," she managed to say before Martha shushed her and hurried Ellie and Mia over to the aisle.

Lydia was shaking for real as she watched the girls begin to walk. And she was still shaking as she started down the aisle herself, stared at by the smiling faces of her family and Gabe's family—with Gabe himself waiting for her at the end of the aisle, dressed in an expensive black suit, his expression thoughtful and sober.

She didn't stop trembling through the readings and hymn and homily and vows. Her voice was a little wobbly as she said, "I do."

Her hand shook as she exchanged rings with Gabe, and she was still shaky as they were pronounced husband and wife.

She was trembling so helplessly as she and Gabe walked up the aisle together afterward that she knew he had to see it.

They ended up back in the dressing room—with Martha, Ellie, and Mia. Gabe reached out for her and pulled her close in what looked like a hug, but he asked in a low murmur, "Are you okay?"

"Yes," she said, trying to smile at him.

"You look like you're about to lose it."

"I know." His arm was tight around her, and she felt like she needed his strength, so she pressed herself against him. She said in a voice as soft as his had been, "I don't know what's wrong with me. I wasn't even nervous. This isn't like me at all."

Gabe pulled away slightly so he could look down at her face. His blue eyes were suddenly questioning. "You're not regretting it already, are you?"

"No!" The response was a little sharper than she'd intended, so she softened it. "I'm not regretting anything. I'm really fine."

The question had disappeared from his face, and his arms tightened around her again. "You're still shaking."

"I know." She buried her face against his jacket, clinging to him in an attempt to pull herself together.

She was never like this. She was never weak and shaky. She was never overly emotional.

Everyone always said she was the most practical, competent person they'd ever met, and marriage certainly wouldn't have changed her.

She knew Gabe had just pulled her into the embrace so he could have a private conversation with her while the others were in the room, but it felt now like he was supporting her.

She kind of liked the feeling.

"Daddy?" a voice came from behind her.

Gabe pulled away and looked down on his daughter, who had moved over to stand near them. "Hi, sweetheart. You looked beautiful and held your flowers perfectly."

"Thank you. Are you done hugging her now?"

"Yes," he said with a low chuckle, reaching down for his daughter. "Now I can hug you."

He hugged the little girl in a tight grip, and the feeling between them was obvious. Lydia felt cold and still trembly after having lost the embrace, but she wasn't about to complain.

She needed Gabe to get to India. She didn't need him in any other way.

They had a small reception at the church, and then Lydia and Gabe drove to Asheville while Ellie went to stay with her grandparents.

Gabe and Lydia were going to spend the weekend in a historic inn in Asheville. Everyone expected them to have a honeymoon, and this was the most low-maintenance thing they could think of.

It wasn't like it was a burden to spend the weekend in an upscale inn. What everyone else expected to happen over the weekend didn't actually have to happen.

The drive went quickly because she and Gabe were talking about plans for their work in India. She was as interested in his business center as she was in her own work, and they actually got a brainstorm for a potential project that could give girls rescued from the brothels training for jobs.

It was in the early stages—just ideas at this point—but Lydia was excited, and she had a great time talking it all out with Gabe, who had the best head for business she'd ever seen.

The inn was a renovation of an old mansion, and it was gorgeous, set amidst the mountain scenery and obviously very expensive.

Lydia felt the first qualm as she pulled her bag out of the car. "They're not going to give us a honeymoon suite or anything, are they?" she asked, gazing up at the white columns and wide porch.

"No. Of course not. I got a two-bedroom suite." Gabe looked surprised, like she'd offended him. "What did you think?"

"Nothing," she said hurriedly, feeling guilty for her question. "I didn't think you would... I mean, sorry."

He gave her a half smile and shook his head.

"Did you have to make up some excuse about why we need two rooms?"

"No. It's none of their business."

She thought about that for a minute and decided he was right. She wasn't sure why she thought it was a big deal. It certainly didn't matter whether the manager of this inn thought they were strange for getting a two-bedroom suite for their honeymoon.

The manager greeted them warmly, and then a bellboy carried up their luggage. The suite was spacious with lovely hardwood floors, a large balcony, and two fireplaces.

Lydia gulped, thinking about how much money Gabe

must have spent on it. She'd have to offer to chip in. Obviously, given the difference in their finances, any contributions she made would be mostly token, but it still felt important to her to make the gesture.

She never wanted Gabe to mistakenly believe she thought his money was hers to use as she liked.

Once all the features of the room and inn were explained, the bellboy left, and Gabe and Lydia stood in the main room, staring at each other.

Tonight was their wedding night.

Lydia couldn't help but be acutely aware of the breadth of Gabe's shoulders, the strength of his jaw, the masculinity in the lines of his body.

He really wouldn't be a bad choice for a wedding night.

Not that they were going to have sex, she reminded herself.

"Which room do you want?" he asked at last, after staring at her the way she'd been him.

"It doesn't matter. They're both lovely."

"Why don't you take the one with the tub then? Assuming you like to take baths, that is."

"I do." She glanced toward the room decorated in shades of blue and rose. "Thank you."

"We can go out for dinner if you want. Or if you're tired, we can just do room service." He was searching her face as if he were trying to read what she was feeling.

"Room service would be great. I'm really tired." She was suddenly very self-conscious—since she definitely didn't want Gabe to know what she was feeling at the moment. She reached for the handle of her suitcase and started rolling it toward her room. "This is a gorgeous suite. Thank you. I hope it wasn't too much."

She was mostly talking to have something to say, but when she glanced back she saw Gabe was frowning. "Of course it wasn't too much."

She didn't know what to say to that, so she just went to hide in her room.

She unpacked a little, and then they ate dinner out on their private veranda. They didn't talk much at first, but it felt comfortable so Lydia enjoyed the quiet.

She actually liked Gabe's company. He seemed just as self-possessed as she was.

So many people she knew—both men and women—felt the need to say anything to fill silences, as if silences were some kind of threat.

Before she realized what she was doing, she asked out of the blue, "What happened with your wife? I mean, Michaela. If you don't mind telling me, of course."

Gabe twitched in surprise, putting down his fork. But he didn't look angry or defensive. Just kind of tired as he gazed out at the mountain scenery. "She didn't want to be married to me anymore."

He made it sound simple, but Lydia was sure it wasn't. "Why not?"

Maybe the question was too pushy, but she was used to asking what she wanted to know.

"I don't know." With a sigh, he turned back to look at her. "She wanted something different out of life. I don't think she wanted to have Ellie at all. Before she was born, we traveled a lot and went out a lot and did a lot of social-izing. It exhausted me, but she thrived on it. Then after

Ellie was born, our lifestyle changed. We had to settle down some, and she didn't want to be that person."

"But how could she..." For once, Lydia thought before she spoke and rephrased to something less blunt. "But surely having Ellie would be worth the change in lifestyle."

"I think so. I think so a thousand times. But evidently Michaela didn't. She finally just left. She fell in a love with a guy who lives the kind of life she wants, so I guess she's got what she wants now."

"Shit," Lydia breathed. "That... sucks."

"Yeah."

"So she doesn't spend much time with Ellie?"

"Not much. It's sporadic. She occasionally wants to see her, but she definitely doesn't want the responsibility."

"I'm really sorry you had to go through all that."

He gave a shrug. "It happens."

She could tell it had been really hard on him, despite his laid-back attitude. "So you never thought about getting married again?"

He shot her a quick look but evidently relaxed at what he saw on her face. "No. It just didn't seem worth it. To go through all that again."

She could understand why he would think that. She would probably think the same thing.

"What about you?" he asked.

"What about me?"

"Why didn't you ever get married?"

She gave a little shrug, kind of like how he had earlier. "It just didn't happen for me. Guys don't even ask me out much anymore."

He chuckled softly. "That might be because you intimi-date them."

"What do you mean?"

"You're so confident and capable—and you don't seem to *need* a man, if you get what I'm saying. You're probably intimidating to most men."

She thought about that for a minute, wondering if he was right. She'd been popular in high school and college, but her appeal as a date seemed to have diminished as the years went by. Then she shrugged it off because it didn't really matter. "I'm married now," she said with a grin, "so I guess we don't have to worry about it anymore."

"I guess not."

They held gazes for a minute before they looked away. The look was confusing somehow. She wasn't sure what to make of it.

Since they were done with their food, Lydia stood up. "It's a great view, but it's a little chilly out here, so I guess I'll head inside."

"Sounds good."

Deciding some alone time would be nice, she went to her room to take a bath.

The tub was huge and jetted, and she had a very nice, relaxing soak. Afterward, she put on lounge pants and a long, belted sweater since it was comfortable but still looked like real clothes. She assumed Gabe was still up, and she didn't want to go out in her pajamas.

Gabe must have showered too because he wore black pajama pants and a white T-shirt. He was standing next to a room service tray, on which a bucket of chilled champagne.

He glanced back at her as she approached. "They sent it up to us," he said, "because they realized it was our honeymoon."

"Oh." She came over to stand beside him, staring at the bottle and crystal flutes. "I guess there's no sense in letting it go to waste."

"Definitely not." He smiled at her as he started to uncork the bottle. "How was your bath?"

"Nice. It's a fantastic tub. This is all so nice."

"Good. I'm glad you like it." His eyes were resting on her face, and she had no idea what the expression meant.

She felt strangely shy as she accepted a glass of champagne and sipped it. Gabe somehow looked even more attractive than he had earlier in his wedding suit. Now he looked relaxed, slightly rumpled, domestic.

Like there was nothing more than a thin layer of fabric keeping her from his body.

She suddenly wanted to touch his body.

She had no idea what was going on with her since she hadn't been inordinately troubled in that way in the past. But now she was actually having to stop herself from reaching out to stroke her hands over his chest.

"What are you thinking?" he asked, sipping his own glass. They were both still standing near the cart.

There was no way in hell she was going to tell him what she was thinking. "Nothing. Just that it's a little strange. To be married, I mean."

"I know." He gave her that small, whimsical smile she liked. "But I think we'll get used to it."

"Yeah. I'm sure we will. Did you call to check on Ellie?"

"She's doing fine. They took her out for pizza for dinner, so that made her happy."

"Good." She couldn't help but notice the dark stubble on his jaw. She couldn't help but wonder how it would feel against her palm. Her eyes drifted down to his lean hips and strong thighs.

She wondered if it ever crossed his mind to be aroused by her. She wasn't any sort of beauty queen, but she wasn't bad-looking. Surely she was capable of turning a man on.

Not that she'd ever tried.

They were married. This was their wedding night. There was really no reason why they shouldn't have sex.

He'd said it was a standing offer.

She could just ask for it.

She opened her mouth, but no sound came out. The words got stuck in her throat.

She was used to saying exactly what she thought, but there was absolutely no way she could bring herself to ask Gabe for sex.

"Well, I think I'm going to try to get some work done," he said, topping off his glass.

"Work? Seriously?"

"Yeah. I can't call or e-mail anyone since they would think it was strange on my wedding night, but I've got other work I can do. Just let me know if you need anything."

She stared at him as he walked across the living area and into his bedroom. He closed the door behind him.

She sighed, slumping down slightly.

What had she expected? They'd agreed they wouldn't

have sex. She could hardly expect him to make a move on her anyway.

Well, some men might have, but not Gabe. He really was a gentleman.

Plus he hadn't seemed all that attracted to her.

Plus he'd gotten really burned before and wasn't going to open himself up with another women.

Plus none of it really mattered because, in a few months, she'd be in India.

She filled her glass of champagne and went to watch TV in her bedroom.

Happy wedding night to her.

CHAPTER 5

LYDIA PUSHED AROUND EGGS IN A PAN AND TRIED TO STAY awake.

It was just six thirty in the morning, but Gabe and Ellie always seemed to get up early, and she thought it would be nice to fix breakfast on their first day back from their "honeymoon" weekend.

The weekend hadn't been miserable. It hadn't been particularly good, but she shouldn't have expected it to be. Gabe worked most of the time although they did spend one afternoon hiking and one afternoon at the Biltmore Estate.

He was still wrapping up stuff with his company, but there was very little she could do herself. She'd made some notes on the possible business project for the rescued girls —maybe jewelry or some sort of craft—and otherwise she read or watched TV or worked out.

It was relaxing, but she was happy when the weekend was over and they returned to Willow Park.

Gabe was perfectly polite, and being in such close quarters with him kept building her attraction for him—but he still sometimes felt like an intimate stranger.

She occasionally tried to bring up more personal topics —like their conversation on the veranda—but he didn't open up like that to her again.

She told herself not to be annoyed or impatient. While it might be nice if they could be friends, it wasn't necessary for their arrangement. And maybe it would just take more time.

Her eggs were starting to scramble when a voice behind her said, "What are you doing?"

She turned around to see Ellie, who was fully dressed in jeans, a snowflake sweater, and two long braids.

No lounging around in her pajamas for Ellie. Lydia felt a little sloppy in her flannel pants, sweatshirt, and unbrushed hair.

"I'm making breakfast," she said, smiling at the girl as brightly as she could. "You like eggs and bacon, don't you?"

Ellie didn't answer. Just peered at the stove top suspiciously.

"Do you want some orange juice?"

"I'll get it." Ellie stepped in front of Lydia on her way to the refrigerator, so Lydia let the girl grab the container and pour for herself.

The girl then went to sit down at the table with her juice.

Trying to think of a topic of conversation, Lydia asked, "So how was your weekend with your grandparents? Did you do anything fun?"

Again, Ellie ignored the question. "Where's Daddy?"

"He was in his room earlier, but I'm sure he'll be down soon."

She'd heard the shower running as she'd been on her way out and had to force from her mind the vision of Gabe naked in the shower.

"Oh."

"So did you do anything fun with your Grandma and Grandpa this weekend?" Lydia tried again, blotting the bacon with a paper towel.

Hopefully, Gabe would be down soon, or her valiant attempt to be nice would go to waste because the food would be cold.

When Ellie didn't answer, Lydia glanced over her shoulder. The girl was frowning down at her glass of juice.

This was hopeless. The girl was never going to like her, and she was absolutely clueless about what to do to change it.

"Ellie, you were asked a question," Gabe said as he walked into the kitchen. There was the slightest sternness in his voice.

Ellie gave a little jerk of surprise at the sight of her father. "Sorry." She took a deep breath and said, not looking at Lydia, "We went to the park and to church and to a big toy store in Dalton."

"Oh, that sounds like fun." Lydia made sure to smile, but she felt uncomfortable because now Ellie would think she'd gotten her in trouble with her dad.

She plated up eggs, toast, and bacon and brought two plates to the table.

"Thanks for cooking," Gabe said, filling a mug with coffee. "You didn't have to do that."

"I'm happy to." She smiled at him and smiled at Ellie even though she was already exhausted for the day.

This marriage-of-convenience thing wasn't as easy as she would have expected. They'd worked all kinds of stuff out beforehand, but there were so many little things she never would have thought to plan for.

Gabe prayed before they started eating, and then she and Gabe talked about what they were going to do today.

Lydia had some more boxes to unpack, and Gabe had some things come up with his company that needed addressing.

"What did you want to do today?" Lydia asked since Ellie was just frowning down at her plate, pushing her food around.

Ellie gave a halfhearted shrug.

"Answer with words," Gabe murmured, that same edge of sternness in his tone.

"I don't know." The girl shot Lydia a look that proved she wasn't happy with her. "Read, I guess."

Lydia started to ask what she was reading, but then she just gave up. No use in torturing the poor girl with a conversation she clearly didn't want to have.

She was spreading jelly on her toast when she noticed Gabe giving Ellie a focused, intentional look.

She wasn't sure what it meant until Ellie turned her fork the right way and started to eat her food instead of pushing it around.

Suddenly Lydia felt so uncomfortable that she had to fight the urge to just leave the room.

She'd never wanted this—this kind of domestic scene, breakfast with a man and child.

It wasn't her, and it wasn't like she was any good at it anyway.

No one looked particularly happy this morning.

Instead of brooding, she let out a breath and told herself it was just temporary.

She could deal with anything as long as there was light at the end of the tunnel.

∽

Later that day, Lydia was organizing books on a big bookcase in the family room.

Gabe had already put some of his books there, but there were plenty of shelves left for hers. She had a fairly large collection, and there was no way she could take them all to India with her, so she might as well get them organized here.

Gabe had taken Ellie out to lunch earlier, and Lydia had used the excuse of being on a roll with unpacking and not wanting to stop, so at least she'd been saved from that uncomfortableness.

Now both Gabe and Ellie were in his office, so Lydia was able to work in peace.

She was, at least until she heard a knock on the door.

She went to answer it and discovered Jessica—Daniel's wife—on the doorstep with a casserole dish.

"Hey," Lydia said, returning Jessica's smile. "Come on in."

"Sorry to just barge in," Jessica explained, carrying the dish into the kitchen and putting it on a counter as she talked. "But I was so focused on making this without messing it up that I didn't even think about calling first until I pulled into the driveway."

Lydia laughed. "It's no problem at all. Did you manage it without messing up?"

"I think so." Jessica pulled away the cover and peered down at what looked like a poppy seed chicken casserole. "It looks okay, doesn't it?"

"It looks great. You didn't have to make it."

"I wanted to. I'm sure you have enough to do, trying to settle in and then all the preparations for going to India." Jessica had dark blond hair, blue eyes, and a tall, slim figure. Right now, however, she was visibly pregnant. She had been in Lydia's grade all through school, but they'd never been really close—since Jessica was quiet and bookish and Lydia had always been involved in sports and student council.

But Lydia liked her. And she knew her. It was nice to be with someone comfortable.

"There's actually not that much for me to be doing yet," Lydia said. She gestured toward the family room, which connected with the kitchen. "I'm finishing up some books, but then the house will be in order. I might do some yard work—there's a bunch of branches and stuff that needs clearing out—but otherwise I'll have to make up things to do."

"This house is gorgeous," Jessica said, looking around at the beautiful kitchen and family room.

"Micah did it a couple of years ago. He always does a good job."

"Yeah. So what are you going to do to fill your time until you leave for India then?"

"I don't know. I might look around for volunteer work. I was actually wondering if I should get some sort of job, but who's going to want to hire me for four months?"

"I don't know. Maybe Gabe has something for you to do. Daniel said he's scrambling to tie up loose ends with his company before the summer."

Lydia hadn't thought about that. She wondered if there might be something she could help him with. She was pretty smart, and she'd been through law school. She wasn't used to having no purpose at all.

"Where is he, by the way?" Jessica added.

"He's in his office with Ellie. You should say hello while you're here."

They walked down the hall toward the office, which was at the back of the house. The door was shut, so Lydia automatically raised her hand to knock on it.

Then she wondered if Jessica would think it was strange that she knocked on a door in her own home.

"Just in case he's on the phone," Lydia murmured, using the only explanation she could think of for the knock.

"Come," Gabe called from inside.

He sounded brusque, businesslike.

Not like an adoring newlywed husband.

Jessica appeared to be hiding a smile when Lydia swung the door open.

Gabe was at his desk, wearing jeans and a T-shirt, staring down at papers that were spread out all over his desk, gripping a pen in his hand.

Ellie was sitting at a chair that was pulled up in front of the credenza, staring down at a spiral-bound notebook opened in front of her, gripping a pen in her hand.

Lydia almost chuckled at how exactly alike they looked. Then she said, "Gabe, Jessica stopped by with a casserole."

Gabe blinked over at them, his eyes appearing more heavy-lidded than normal, as if he could barely pull his focus away from his work. "Oh. Thank you. Hi, Jessica." He put his pen down and started to get up.

"Hi. Please don't get up. I can't stay long. Just thought I'd save you all from the trouble of fixing dinner."

"We appreciate it," Lydia said.

"Yes, thank you." Gabe glanced over at his daughter, who was still focused on writing in her notebook. "Ellie, say hello to Mrs. Duncan and thank her for the dinner she made for us."

Ellie looked up and then smiled. "Thank you!" She sounded almost genuine. Much more genuine than she ever sounded with Lydia.

"You're welcome. What are you working on so hard in here?"

"I'm writing a story."

"Is that for school?" Jessica asked.

"No. My school is over until after Christmas. I'm writing a story for fun."

"Oh, wow. That sounds great. Maybe you'll let me read it when you're done."

"Maybe."

Ridiculously, Lydia was almost jealous over this pleasant conversation. Why couldn't Ellie respond to her that way? She was the one who had to live with her, after all.

She smothered a sigh and showed Jessica to the door.

"That looks familiar," Jessica said, nodding back toward the office and idly rubbing her rounded belly.

"What does?"

"Him. In the office that way with the door closed. Not that Daniel had a daughter with him, but still..." Jessica sighed. "Don't let him stay in there all the time."

Lydia felt a strange little jump in her chest. "What do you mean?"

"Maybe I'm wrong, but if he's anything like Daniel, he'll want to hide in there. Don't let him hide from you."

Lydia suddenly felt uncomfortable again. Jessica didn't have a weird marriage of convenience. She had a wonderful marriage with a man who adored her—whose adoration was obvious for all to see. Lydia wasn't in the same situation. And the truth was, she didn't mind if Gabe hid in his office since it meant she didn't have to try to make pleasant conversation and pretend that their situation was normal.

The following week, Lydia was doing some research on jewelry making in India when Gabe knocked on her bedroom door.

Her bedroom was large with a sunny nook where she'd put a comfortable chair and her laptop. It was a very nice place to work.

She'd been spending a lot of time there since it felt private, like she could relax and just be herself.

The rest of the time, she was trying to cook meals, take Ellie on errands, and clean up around the house. Gabe wasn't a slob or anything, but he was obviously really busy with his work. Lydia wasn't. She thought it was reasonable to make an extra effort right now, just to prove that she was doing her part in the marriage. And Gabe seemed to accept it without question.

Lydia put down her laptop when Gabe came in though. He was carrying his phone.

"I've got to go to Raleigh this evening," he said without preamble. "We've run into a bit of a snag with work."

"Okay," she said, straightening up. "When will you be back?"

"Tomorrow. It will just be a short trip. I'd rather not take Ellie since I'll be working the whole time. Do you mind her staying here?"

"Oh." Lydia blinked, her stomach dropping at the thought of being with the girl on her own for a day and a half. "Okay. Yeah, I guess that would be okay."

"Good. Thanks. I'm going to pack and take off right away."

"Where is Ellie now?"

"She's up in her room reading. I'll go up and tell her before I leave."

"Okay."

Lydia didn't like this idea. At all. She didn't like to be solely responsible for a child's welfare. And she definitely didn't like trying to take care of a girl like Ellie, who obviously wanted nothing to do with her.

But Gabe seemed to think it was important that he leave. He seemed to think that it was natural that she'd watch his daughter while he went off on business.

And Lydia had no good reason not to do it since she had nothing else pressing to do.

In their preparations for marriage, they'd agreed that Gabe had primary responsibility for Ellie, but Lydia would help when she could.

She could now.

So before she knew it, she and Ellie were standing on the porch together, watching Gabe drive away in his fancy car.

Lydia took a deep breath and looked down at the girl.

She was wearing the braids again, and she was frowning as her dad disappeared down the street.

"Well," Lydia said, trying to sound cheerful. "Looks like it's just you and me. Do you want to do something fun this afternoon? We can go to the library or shopping or something."

Ellie stared up at her with those dark blue eyes. "I'm going to read."

Lydia sighed. "Okay."

At seven the following evening, Lydia was just about at the end of her rope.

She'd done everything she could think of to bond with Ellie. She'd taken her out to eat for dinner the day before and breakfast this morning. She'd taken her to the library and to the bakery for donuts. She'd tried to play three different games. She'd asked about the books the girl was reading and the story she was writing and the friends she'd had in school. She'd tried to make a game of cleaning the kitchen so Ellie might want to join her.

And nothing. The girl hadn't even smiled.

Lydia had gotten so desperate that she'd called up her mom for advice.

"She just doesn't like me," Lydia said for about the fifth time. She'd rehearsed the past two days, and the frustrated helplessness was catching up to her. Her voice broke on the last word. "She's mostly a well-behaved girl. She's never nasty, and she obeys her father really well. But she doesn't like me—no matter what I do."

"You've got to give her some time," her mother said. "It's only been a couple of weeks."

"Yeah, but it's been months since I got together with Gabe. I wouldn't mind if there was slow progress, but there's no progress at all. I don't know what to do. I'm just no good with kids."

"You've always said that, but I've never known why. You do fine with kids."

"No, I don't. I never know what to say to them."

"You just haven't spent a lot of time around them, but they've always liked you fine."

"But Ellie doesn't. Don't you have any suggestions on how I can talk to her or what I can do?"

"I'm sorry, honey, I don't know what to tell you—except kids aren't alien creatures. They're people. Treat her like a person. If it were you in her situation, how would you want to be treated?"

Lydia sighed and slumped down on the couch, stretching her legs out and closing her eyes. "I just don't know. I've never been in her situation, and I'm so exhausted now I can't even think."

"It just feels overwhelming now because it's new to you and you're not used to it. It will get easier. I promise. She's your family now. Try to start thinking about her that way, and she'll eventually warm up."

Lydia didn't reply to that. Ellie didn't feel like family, any more than Gabe did. That was part of why it was so hard, and it was something she couldn't tell her mother.

"What does Gabe say about it?" her mom asked.

"Nothing."

"You mean you haven't told him you're having trouble with her?"

"I'm not having trouble with her. I mean, it's not like she's really being bad."

"But he still needs to know. How does she act when he's around?"

"Better. She'll answer me and say thank you when he's around. It's not like she's ever friendly."

"Well, tell him. He'll want to know you're so upset about it. The two of you can figure out something to do."

"I don't want to go and whine to him about his daughter."

"It's not whining. It's part of life. If you're building a family together, you all need to work together to deal with anything that comes up."

Lydia swallowed and bit back an immediate objection.

Her mother's tone softened as she added, "You've got to work together, honey, or a marriage can never work."

"Yeah. I know." Lydia opened her eyes and realized her mother was right.

It didn't matter why or how she'd married Gabe. It was still a marriage. And Ellie and her happiness were important. They needed to somehow make this work.

When he got home, she'd talk to him. It would be fine. They were two reasonable people, and they could figure out a way to make this marriage successful.

~

Gabe didn't get back until almost midnight.

Lydia put Ellie to bed at nine, and she stayed awake in her bedroom, waiting. At ten, when he still hadn't arrived, she'd gotten ready for bed, but she kept the light on and read, listening for the sounds of Gabe returning.

Maybe she should just wait until the next morning, but she'd steeled herself to have the conversation tonight, so she wanted to just get it done.

Finally, she heard the garage door open and his car pull in. She waited and heard his footsteps on the stairs. They kept going up to the third floor, so he must be checking on Ellie.

Hopefully the girl was asleep.

He didn't stay up there long, so she must have been sleeping. Lydia waited when she heard the floor of the hallway creak outside her bedroom.

Maybe he'd check in with her to let her know he was back and see how things had gone.

The light was on in her room, after all, so it would be a polite thing to do.

He didn't though. After a moment, she heard the footsteps continue on to his room.

She let out a breath and stood up.

She wore a pair of red cotton pajama pants and a matching tank top. Since it was a little chilly and she felt too exposed, she pulled on a hoodie to cover her arms and shoulders before she left the room.

Her hair was rather tousled, but she didn't really care.

She wasn't trying to look good. She wanted to have a reasonable conversation with Gabe.

His door was half-open, so she tapped on it and pushed it open farther.

He was in the process of pulling his shirt off, and she froze at the sight of his broad, well-developed back and his very fine ass in the trousers he still wore.

He turned around quickly at her knock, holding his shirt in his hands.

"Sorry," she said quickly. "The door was…"

His chest was very nice too. She trailed off as her eyes lingered on the well-developed muscles and scattering of dark hair.

"It's fine. I thought you were in bed." He was staring at her too, and he hadn't moved, not even to put his shirt down.

"Yeah. I mean, no, I was just reading."

Lydia started breathing a little quickly at the sight of him half-dressed this way. In his bedroom. In their house.

"How did things go?" he asked, finally realizing he was still holding his shirt and tossing it toward the closet.

She took a few steps into the room. "Fine. It was… it was okay."

His brows drew together. "Is something wrong?"

She was flushed and breathless from seeing him like

this, but she had enough brain capacity to realize this wasn't what he was asking. "Not really. Not wrong, really. It's just that—"

"Is Ellie okay?"

"She's fine," Lydia replied, just slightly sharp. She was trying to explain, if he'd just let her get the words out. "It's not that. It's just that it's been kind of hard to... to do everything myself."

That wasn't exactly what she'd wanted to say, but it was certainly the truth.

He frowned and stepped closer to her. "I thought you said it was fine to watch her while I was gone."

"I did. I mean, it was. Although we might want to talk about it some more since you seemed to expect me to without question, and that's not always going to work for me. But—"

"What do you mean I expected you to without question? I asked you. What else could I have done?" His body had tensed up, and his voice was edged with annoyance.

Lydia was suddenly annoyed too. She hadn't been very lucid with her explanation, but he didn't need to immediately take offense this way. She had a valid point. "You could have run the possibility by me before it was a done deal. You were practically out the door when you asked me. What could I have said but yes?"

"You could have said no. What else did you need to do?" He'd moved even closer to her, big and tense and quietly angry.

She sucked in a breath at the implication. "Just because I'm not working right now doesn't mean my time is entirely yours to use. I didn't marry you to become your babysitter or housekeeper, you know."

She wasn't the kind of person who got angry easily. Annoyed, yes. Angry, no. So she had no idea why she was so angry right now. But she was practically shaking with it, wanting to claw the condescending, impatient look off his face.

"Damn it," he bit out. "When did I ever say you should be my housekeeper or babysitter?"

"You didn't have to say it. But for the past week I've done the housework and made the meals and watched your daughter. We'd agreed we would split things up equally, and that's not what is happening."

He was almost choking on some sort of outrage. "You offered to do all that. If you didn't want to, then why the hell did you offer?"

"I was trying to be nice. And you haven't showed the slightest bit of appreciation or reciprocation."

"I said thank you. What else did you expect?"

Their voices weren't loud, but they were both angry, and he was very close to her now.

She could reach out and touch him. Ridiculously, she was still overwhelmed with that physical attraction—even more so now that he was so visceral, so passionate, so real.

Not distant at all—angry and in her face this way.

"I expected this to be a partnership," she snapped. "And that's not what it is. I feel like I'm the only one making any effort here, and I'm not going to keep making efforts if you're not willing to do your share."

"And it never occurred to you to open your mouth and

let me know you weren't happy about things?" He was breathing heavily, and his cheeks were slightly flushed.

She wanted so much for him to kiss her that she had to clench her fingers at her sides.

"I'm opening my mouth now," she said. Her voice cracked slightly, and she realized she needed to leave— right now—before she did something incredibly stupid.

And humiliating.

So she just turned on her heel and walked out of the room.

"Lydia." His hoarse voice followed her out the hall. "Don't—"

She didn't hear the rest because she'd closed her bedroom door behind her.

She rarely fought. With anyone. She occasionally rubbed people the wrong way, but she always apologized and made an effort to make things better. With some work, she'd always gotten along well with everyone in her life, and any brief disagreements she'd been able to smooth over with honesty and a warm smile.

Her fight with Gabe kept her awake for a long time.

This marriage was supposed to help both of them and not demand too much.

But it was demanding a lot more from her than she'd ever expected.

CHAPTER 6

Lydia didn't sleep very well that night, and she was wide awake at 4:50 the following morning, stewing about her marriage and how weird and awkward things seemed to be with Gabe. So finally she just got up and headed outside for a run.

She would have preferred to swim, but the indoor pool she used wouldn't open for three more hours, so running would have to do.

She alternated running, jogging, and walking for an hour and a half, and she was feeling absolutely exhausted but better when she came back to the house.

Things were fine. This weirdness wouldn't last forever. Soon they'd be in India and she could focus on her work. She needed to try not to be impatient or frustrated with the way things were now. No sense in arguing with Gabe—about anything really. They needed to think practically and not with their emotions. Things would be a lot simpler that way.

In the scheme of things, her relationship with Gabe

didn't matter all that much. It was merely a means to an end. So she could make the effort to get along with him even if the dynamics weren't exactly what she thought was best.

So she felt reenergized as she limped into the kitchen for water, breathing heavily and flushed from the exercise. It was kind of chilly outside, so she wasn't soaked in sweat, but she felt hot in the house, so she took off the long-sleeved shirt she wore over a fitted T-shirt.

She jerked to a stop when she saw Gabe was in the kitchen, standing in front of the coffeepot.

He wore a pair of pajama pants and nothing else.

And *nothing* else.

His back was to her, and she stared at the broad, strong lines of his back tapering down to his waist and hips.

He was only semiregular about working out, so every inch of his body wasn't perfectly toned. But he was built big and masculine, and even the slight imperfections—the slight love handles just above his waistband—made him seem realer, more human, more touchable.

Damn, did she want to touch him.

She was hit with the desire after about ten seconds of staring at him, in the space of time it took for him to register her presence and turn around.

"Good morning," she said, trying to sound natural. Instead, she sounded stiff, and her voice cracked slightly. She was still breathing heavily from her run, but now her blood was pulsing with something else.

His blue eyes ran up and down the length of her. "Good morning."

She walked farther into the kitchen since there was

something here she was supposed to be getting—although she couldn't remember what it was at the moment. She couldn't tear her eyes away from Gabe—his sleep-tousled hair, his bristly jaw, his bare chest. The pulsing in her body only intensified as she got closer to him.

On her run, she'd just reminded herself that this marriage—this man—wasn't what was most important in her life.

But suddenly he felt very important. Like he was consuming her body and mind.

"You're up early," he said, taking the mug from beneath the one-cup brewer and taking a sip of black coffee. He looked kind of tired, but maybe it was just because he hadn't fully woken up yet.

"Yeah." She made herself turn away from him because she was so overwhelmed with visceral hunger. It was ridiculous. She was a mature, reasonable woman who was perfectly capable of controlling any stray lust she happened to feel.

She stared at the refrigerator blankly until she remembered she'd come in here to get water. So she opened the door and stared inside until her mind registered where the bottles of water were.

Get it together. Get it together. It's just a guy without a shirt.

"Are you still pouting?" Gabe asked from behind her, his voice slightly skeptical.

Her mind snapped back into focus, and she whirled around, forgetting all of her self-lectures about being reasonable. "Pouting? I'm not *pouting*. I was never *pouting*."

He reacted to her sharp tone immediately, his shoulders

stiffening visibly. "Fine, whatever you want to call it. Are you still pissed?"

"I wasn't pissed until you used that offensive, condescending word."

He sucked in an indignant breath. "It was just a question."

"It wasn't just a question. You chose to use the word 'pout' as if I am a child and my concerns are trivial and petty." She was so irrationally annoyed with him that she was practically shaking with it.

For a moment she saw herself as if from a distance, and she could see how absurd it was to react this way. But she couldn't seem to help it.

Gabe was just making her mad.

She evidently made him mad too—even though he was normally so laid-back. He stepped closer to her, seeming to absorb in his body all the heat and tension in the room. "You're imagining things," he gritted out. "If you're going to overanalyze every word I say, we're never going to be able to have a rational conversation."

"So now you're saying I'm irrational?"

Shit. She was doing nothing but making it worse. She needed to just shut up.

He bit off a frustrated groan. "I'm not saying you're irrational. I'm not saying you're a child. I won't say anything at all if you don't want me to."

She consciously tempered her tone although she was still bristling with annoyance. "Don't act like this is all my fault. I'm sorry if I'm being overly sensitive. I'm not usually this way, but this is new to me and maybe I'm not feeling entirely secure. But the problem here is not just on me. You've got to try to think about me too."

"I do think about you." His voice was still gruff, but it was lower now. He was still very close to her. So close she could reach out and touch him.

"Do you?" She took a ragged breath and tightened her hands into fists at her sides so she wouldn't lift them to his chest.

She'd never known it was possible to want to both stroke and shake someone at the exact same time.

"Of course." He lifted one hand and planted it on the refrigerator behind her in a strangely possessive gesture that trapped her with his body. "What exactly do you want from me?"

She was panting audibly, visibly, but she couldn't possibly control it. Her body hummed with feeling even as her heart and mind throbbed with an emotional turmoil she just wasn't used to. "Nothing. I don't want anything from you."

That wasn't true. It wasn't even close to true.

He leaned in even closer, so intense that she could hardly believe this was the same man she'd married. "I said I was sorry about last night."

"Did you?" She honestly couldn't remember if he'd said the words, but he sure hadn't acted sorry last night. Without thinking, she put one hand on his chest, unable to stop herself from touching the warm substance of his body. "It didn't really seem like you understood what I was trying to say."

He let out a rough breath. "I didn't. Not last night. But I thought about it all night, and I *am* sorry. You're right that I was just assuming you'd be there when I needed you—like you were some kind of convenience to me. I was going to apologize this morning, but things kind of went... awry."

She let out a huff of amusement, relaxing as she met his eyes again. "Yeah. I was going to apologize too. I think it's just..." She trailed off, suddenly conscious that she wasn't just touching him. She was rubbing her hand just slightly, feeling the firm flesh, the coarse hair, the...

"Just what?" he asked thickly. His body radiated a kind of tension that seemed to match the tension in her own body.

"Just..." She had absolutely no idea what she was going to say. "Hard."

He was hard. Deliciously hard beneath her hand. Her breathing accelerated as she stared at her fingers against his chest.

He was breathing faster too. He looked down at how she was touching him.

"Being married, I mean," she managed to explain so he wouldn't think she'd been talking about anything else.

"Yeah." His voice was slightly abrupt and so was his touch as he removed her hand from his body. "No one said marriage was easy." He turned his back on her to pick up his mug of coffee. It must be lukewarm by now.

She blinked at his back since it had felt like they were about to make a connection—come to a real understanding —and he'd suddenly pulled away from it. "I know it's not easy," she began. "I think we can make it work if we both try. I'm sorry that I—"

"It's fine," he said gruffly, still not looking at her. "I've got to go get dressed."

He started to leave the kitchen as she stared at his retreating back. "But, Gabe," she said, feeling ludicrously disappointed. "I think we need to talk about—"

"We will. Later."

Then he was gone, heading up the stairs. Quickly.

And she was left in the kitchen by herself, with a lot of things she wanted to say about how they could work on their marriage.

And a lot of things she wanted to do—with him—that she wasn't able to do.

Lydia felt weird and awkward for the rest of the day. She went to shower—taking a longer one than normal—and came down to breakfast with the resolve to be particularly nice and patient.

She couldn't control how Gabe acted, but she could control how she acted, and she was going to try to make this marriage work.

They had breakfast with Ellie, who looked at both of them suspiciously and finally asked if they were fighting—which both of them vehemently denied.

Then Lydia was purposefully cheerful about their plans for the day—which included Gabe working, Ellie reading and writing in his office with him, and Lydia going to help her parents clean out their basement.

Gabe seemed basically normal after that morning, but it still felt like they hadn't quite worked things out.

It grated on her. That he'd pulled away when they could have come to a better understanding. She was still thinking about it after she took a bath that evening and got into bed.

She was sure she could control the lust—that was a physical response and was probably heightened because she'd never been in such close quarters with a man before. But they had to work out how they would function together if they were going to make this marriage work.

Finally, she couldn't relax until she took a proactive step, so she got out of bed and headed to his room. She could see the light was still on from the crack at the bottom of the door, so she assumed he was still awake.

She knocked on the door.

She gave a little gasp when it swung open in about thirty seconds and Gabe stood in the doorway, dressed only in a pair of boxers.

She gulped—afraid it was audible but unable to stop herself. She was hit once again with that wave of visceral attraction, the likes of which she'd never experienced before.

"Sorry," she managed to say. "I didn't think… I mean, I thought you weren't in bed yet. The light was on."

"I was about to get in bed." His eyes slid down her body, taking in her soft pajama pants and tank top and lingering on where one of the straps was slipping down her shoulder. "What's the matter?"

"Nothing. I just wanted to… I felt like we didn't quite finish our conversation this morning. About getting along, I mean. And it was bugging me. I really want this marriage to work."

"I do too." Something had tightened in his body, in his expression. "And we can talk about it. But not now."

She frowned. "Why not now?"

His voice was deliciously thick as he said, "Because you're not wearing many clothes right now, and it's very distracting."

She glanced down at herself in faint surprise and then up at him. She suddenly realized that the tension she sensed in him was arousal.

Arousal. He was aroused. By her.

A thrill of excitement, pleasure, and satisfaction washed over her with this knowledge.

It was a relief. And felt right. That he was attracted to her too.

"Oh," she said, realizing he was waiting for her to reply. "Sorry. I didn't…"

"I know you didn't realize it. I'm sorry we can't talk now. But I want to respect your wishes about not having sex, and that means I have to walk away when I'm getting too…" He cleared his throat and glanced away from her. "Turned on."

"Oh." She sucked in a shaky breath, suddenly swept with the same kind of hunger she'd felt that morning. He was wearing almost nothing. And he was big and warm and masculine and strong. And *Gabe.* "Well maybe…" She trailed off again although she'd always considered herself quite articulate in the past.

His eyes shot back to her face. "Maybe what?"

"Maybe sex isn't a problem. I mean, maybe we can reconsider. After all, we're married—"

Gabe didn't even bother trying to respond with words. He just pushed the door shut behind her and closed the small gap between them, his handsome, strained face leaning in toward hers.

If she had thought about it, Lydia would have expected him to be slow and gentle at first, had thought he might try to ease them into this—since it was the first time they were together, and she was entirely new to this. But his mouth and hands were immediately hot, hungry, and needy, and as he moved his mouth roughly over hers, he clutched her almost painfully.

But somehow it was exactly what she wanted. She responded, feeling an answering hunger spring up in her own body. She pressed herself against him, clawed at his back, opened her mouth to his seeking tongue and then tried to outmaneuver it with her own.

When he finally lowered his lips from her mouth to her neck, Lydia was breathless and unsteady. Gasping, she heard herself whispering, "Gabe." As if his name had some sort of power in this room. Her heart was still drumming painfully, and she thought she could feel an answering rhythm from him as her breasts pressed into his chest.

His hands were stroking her back. Then lower, cupping her butt. And he was pushing her pelvis against his. Rocking his already full erection into her rhythmically.

And it was all happening so fast. She'd expected a little more preparation time. Lydia felt a stirring of anxiety, but the need she felt far outweighed it.

She let her head fall back in an attempt to suck in some air without breathing in his heat and body. "I'm not on birth control," she panted, trying to pull herself together.

"I've got condoms." Gabe might have been trying to rein himself in, but he wasn't doing a very good job. He bent over and lowered his face to the deep neckline of her tank top, licked the line down her cleavage.

She groaned as he lifted a hand to cup her over her shirt, her head falling back again but this time involuntarily. She could feel arousal building between her legs, could hardly believe this was happening.

Feeling her legs shaking a little, she still managed to ask, "Why do you have condoms?"

The hands that had been fondling her breasts moved down to grab the bottom of her top. Then he lifted it up over her head. Lydia had to release her hold on him in order to get it off all the way. "I was hoping you'd change your mind," he admitted, slightly wry, even as he stared at her naked torso hungrily.

For some reason his answer filled her with affection. Without thinking, she reached up and took his face in her hands to pull him down into another deep kiss.

Even though she had initiated the kiss, Gabe's urgency soon took over. It felt like he was drinking her in, swallowing her down whole. His mouth was ravenous and merciless. But Lydia didn't mind. She felt the same way too and more so when he slid down her pajama pants and underwear, leaving her naked.

She thought she would have wanted to go slow, but she didn't. Her nipples were hard already, and they chafed deliciously against his firm body. "Gabe," she gasped when she turned her head aside to breathe. "I want you so much."

"I want you too." His arousal was pushing into her now more insistently, and each time he thrust against her, her inner muscles clenched possessively.

She realized it was true. He really, really wanted her—in some sort of primal way.

With his hands on her hips, he lifted her up, and she instinctively wrapped her legs around him. This move brought her hot center into contact with his belly, and she rubbed herself against him shamelessly.

He moaned as she moved against him, and then he pushed her hips into him more tightly. He pressed his face into her hair. "Fuck, you're amazing, Lydia."

She wasn't in the habit of using or hearing such language, but it felt natural to hear it in this context for some reason, and the sentiment filled her chest even more fully.

He walked them both over to the bed and then bent over to lay her down. He gazed at her for a minute as she sprawled naked on the bed and waited for him.

His gaze was so intent and so deep that she started to squirm. Smiling at him awkwardly, she said, "You're the one who's done this before. I hope you know what happens next."

He released a short burst of amusement and slid down his underwear. As she saw him strip, Lydia felt a lump of fear reemerge in her throat. In this lull from the momentum of desire, she realized what was happening.

She was going to have sex. With her husband. For the first time.

She was going to have sex with Gabe.

She closed her eyes momentarily to process this shift. When she opened them, Gabe was naked in front of her, his erection hard and prominent, almost at the level of her eyes.

Her eyes widened as she stared at him, and she even felt her mouth fall open a little. Then she shifted her gaze up to Gabe's amused face. "Something wrong?" he asked dryly.

Lydia gulped. "Not a thing. I'm game if you are."

He laughed. "I'm definitely game."

He joined her on the bed, moving over her, his body fitting against hers in a way that felt strangely natural. He kissed her again. Traced his hands urgently over her body. Ended up slipping his fingers between her legs, testing to see if she was ready for him.

She was ready.

Just before he started nudging her legs farther apart, he shook his head roughly and muttered, "Condom."

He reached into the drawer of the nightstand to grab one, and he tore it open clumsily and then fumbled a bit as he rolled it on.

Then he was with her again, moving over her, parting her legs to make room for his body.

After kissing her, his teeth nipping her lower lip, he asked huskily, "Are you sure about this?"

Lydia reached up and splayed her hands out against the back of his head, tangling her fingers in his thick hair. He was supporting himself on his forearms, and his upper body was so close to hers that their chests were brushing against each other. "I'm sure. I haven't done this before, but I know what I'm doing. So just get going."

Gabe got going.

He entered her slowly, carefully, his hand shaking slightly as he lined himself up. He felt big and firm and too tight, but her body stretched and moved to accommodate him.

She'd heard it might hurt, but it didn't. Not really. It was just so tight she was panting loudly in response.

Gabe had his eyes squeezed shut, and she suddenly realized that he was trying to retain his control. She waited silently, without moving until he opened his eyes and gazed down at her.

"Okay?" he asked briefly, a battle going on in his eyes.

"Yeah."

"Does it hurt?"

"Not really. Kind of uncomfortable." She took a deep breath. "It will get better." She rocked her hips up into him a little, testing out the sensations.

"Tell me when you're ready," he said thickly, turning his head as he struggled to control himself.

It must have been a long time for him—if he hadn't had sex since he got divorced.

"I'm ready," she said, the feelings adjusting so that, while still a little uncomfortable, there was something else compelling her to move.

He started to thrust, trying so hard to remain slow and steady that he was actually shaking. She pumped her hips up to meet him every time he sank deep into her, and it took a minute or two for them to establish a rhythm.

"Yeah," she breathed when they started to move in sync. "That's… kind of… good."

He made a huffing sound, his hot eyes never leaving her face and body.

She felt little bursts of pleasure with each stroke, and her body began to tune itself into their pattern. Soon her motion was instinctive, automatic, an innate drive toward release and completion. She suddenly wondered if she might even be able to come although that was never in her expectations for her first time.

She just needed a little more time.

But time was something Gabe didn't have. He was already sweating profusely, and his eyes were almost glazed over in his struggle to not lose control. "Lydia. Fuck, I can't…"

"It's good," she said. "Let go."

She didn't know if Gabe made a conscious decision in response to her words, or if he simply lost the remaining shreds of his self-restraint. But the steady rhythm he'd been holding abruptly fell apart, and he started driving into her harder, faster.

Little whimpers started forcing their way from her throat, but they were from pleasure as much as from effort. It was still good although now she believed it would be over before she could reach orgasm.

It was fine. It was still good. She watched Gabe's face as her body moved with his. Saw how much he needed this. Thrilled at the reality of it.

"Lydia," Gabe ground out, his face so close she could feel his breath on her cheek. "Can't hold back… much longer." He moved his arms until his forearms were under her neck. Then he adjusted his knees so that he could get more leverage to thrust.

"Don't hold back," she choked, feeling an orgasm starting to build but knowing it would be too slow. "Come, Gabe." She clutched at his back, loving how real and solid he felt under her hands. "I want you to come." Her whole body was jostled by the momentum of every thrust, and the bed beneath them was squeaking just a little.

He let out a frustrated groan and tried to slow himself down, but she tightened around him purposefully until he fell out of rhythm. His eyes were closed again, and his incoherent grunts were hot and primitive.

Lydia had never felt so powerful. So desired. So needed. She shuddered with delight—from the impact of this knowledge as much as from the friction inside of her. "It's good, Gabe," she gasped. "It's so good."

He gave a few final pushes inside her, then bit out her name as he froze with his climax. Then she felt the tighter spasms of his release inside her. Saw raw, naked pleasure replace the frustrated hunger and effort on his face.

He collapsed on top of her when the contractions finally ceased, the whole weight of his body all at once pushing her into the mattress. It was a little uncomfortable, but it was also so good. She tightened her arms around him and held him as close to her as she could make him.

Neither one spoke for a long stretch of time until his weight finally became too much for her. She shifted a little, and Gabe immediately reacted. Raised himself up and gently, very carefully pulled out of her, taking care with the condom.

Then he flopped down beside her again and gave her a wry look.

"Surely you didn't expect me to come too," she said with a little smile.

He narrowed his eyes. "It's been known to happen."

She laughed softly. "It was my first time. I really enjoyed it. I had no unrealistic expectations."

"I'm not sure they were unrealistic."

"If you say so." She was still smiling when he rolled over

98

closer to her. She loved how soft and relaxed he looked now. "What are you doing?"

"Proving a point," he murmured, just before he kissed her. The kiss was slow, without the urgency of before. Then he moved lower, lavishing leisurely attention on her body with his mouth and hands. He spent a while on her neck and shoulders before finally descending to her breasts.

His mouth was creative and skillful as he suckled one of her nipples, and she was soon wriggling and pushing up against him. "I think you can move on," she gasped.

"To where?" he teased, raising his head to look down at her with an amused glint she'd only seen occasionally in his face.

"You know where." She was having to fight not to squirm since she was so aroused.

"You could tell me."

Feeling a matching teasing, she wasn't going to cave so easily. Instead, she brought his hand down from one of her breasts and settled it between her legs.

He chuckled and slipped the hand between her thighs, and his fingers teased her open. "Is this what you want?" Sinking one finger inside her, he pumped it in and out experimentally. When she bucked up at the jolt of pleasure, a second finger joined the first.

"Oh, yeah," she gasped, feeling the semi-halted momentum of her earlier interrupted arousal returning with his skillful stimulation. As he thrust his fingers into her, angling them in exactly the right way, she started rocking her hips into the motion.

His mouth latched on to one of her breasts, and his free

hand moved to the curves of her butt to help guide the motion of her pelvis. Lydia grabbed at his head and held it down to her chest, feeling the multiple pleasures coming together.

"Oh, Gabe, please don't stop." She was now jerking just as erratically as Gabe had been earlier. She was so close, almost there, started making helpless little sounds in time with his pumping.

Then he moved his other hand from her butt. Slid it forward toward where his fingers were sliding in and out of her. Massaged her for only a moment, pushing her over the edge.

She opened her mouth in a silent exclamation of pleasure as her body spasmed around his fingers, and one of her legs twitched so much that she accidentally clobbered him in the hip with her knee. "Sorry," she gasped as the contractions started to ease. Her body was trembling, but she felt a wash of pure satisfaction.

Gabe shook his head, smiling a little, and rubbed his hip where she had knocked into it. "I think I'll survive." After a few last soothing strokes, he pulled his hand out from between her legs.

She giggled, squeezing her thighs together over the lingering sensations. "That was amazing."

He looked rather pleased at her words and stretched out beside her, pulling her closer with one of his arms. "Good. You're pretty good yourself."

"I wasn't expecting it to be nearly so good."

He stiffened slightly. "Why wouldn't you think it would be good?"

"Nothing about you," she said quickly. "Just sex in general. Especially the first time."

He gently stroked her hair. "I think we can do even better. I usually have more control than that. It's been a long time for me, and you've been making me crazy with lust for a while now."

"Really?" She looked up at his face with a pleased smile, realizing he was serious.

"Yeah."

"Well, I've kind of wanted you too."

"Good." He kissed her hair with a sigh.

She felt close to him—closer than she'd ever felt to a man before. She wanted to snuggle against him. But she was suddenly hit with the knowledge that it wasn't always going to be like this between them.

They were headed for India where they would both pour themselves into their work. She wasn't even going to live with him a lot of the time since he had to spend the school year in the States.

She had to be careful about getting ideas that weren't practical, weren't smart, weren't part of their arranged agreement.

So she made herself pull away from his warm body, no matter how much she wanted to be close to it. "Thank you," she said, sitting up in bed and pulling a sheet up to cover her breasts when she felt kind of self-conscious.

"You're welcome," he said, blinking slightly in what might be surprise. "Thank *you*."

"I think I can sleep now, so I'm going to head back to bed."

He nodded, pulling back from her slightly. "Okay. Sure."

Something felt awkward between them for the first time, but she ignored it because she had to get away before she started having daydreams that would never come true.

She grabbed her pajamas from the floor and pulled them on, feeling suddenly so sore between her legs that she winced.

"Are you okay?" he asked, raising himself up.

"I'm fine," she said quickly, limping to the door. "A little sore. Nothing too bad. It was great."

He stared at her, revealing nothing. Feeling like he'd pulled back in some way. "Yeah. Goodnight."

"Night."

Then she was finally out of the door and back in the safety of her room.

She felt weird and shaking and like she hadn't handled things right, but she wasn't sure what else she could do.

They weren't in love. They would never be that way.

They could have sex if they both wanted to, but she didn't get to spend the night in his arms.

CHAPTER 7

THE NEXT MORNING, LYDIA WOKE UP GROGGY AND WITH A heaviness in the pit of her stomach, and it took her a few minutes to remember why.

She'd had sex with Gabe last night, and now she felt weird about it.

There was no reason to feel that way. They were married. They could have sex if they both wanted to, and clearly both of them had last night. She tried to talk herself back into her normal reasonable perspective but didn't succeed.

Her head felt so fuzzy that she pulled a sweatshirt on over her pajamas and went downstairs for coffee. She was a little sore between her legs, and each time she felt the pang of pain, she remembered why, making her feel a little heavier.

The heaviness only increased when she realized that Gabe and Ellie were already up and in the kitchen. She heard them before she turned the corner to see.

"Good morning," she said brightly, determined not to let Gabe see that she felt uncomfortable about the night before.

"Morning," he said, glancing back from the stove where he appeared to be making pancakes. He was wearing a sweatshirt and pajama pants, just like her, and his hair was rumpled and eyelids heavier than normal. But his blue eyes were sharp as they rested on her.

She smiled breezily and turned to Ellie, who was seated at the table with an open book in front of her. "Good morning, Ellie."

The girl mumbled, "Good morning," without looking up.

Lydia sighed. Exhibit One that sex didn't fix relationships. Things weren't any better this morning than they'd been yesterday.

When she realized that Gabe was still watching her, she smiled in his direction and headed for the refrigerator, mostly for something to do. She looked inside for a moment before her eyes landed on the orange juice. Then decided that was as good an excuse for opening the refrigerator as anything else.

She grabbed the carton, closed the door, and turned around—only to discover that Gabe was standing directly in front of her.

She gasped involuntarily and stared up at him.

He leaned in closer. "Is everything okay?" he murmured, barely audible. Obviously, he didn't want his daughter to hear the question.

"Of course." She kept her voice just as low, but she wished he weren't standing quite so close.

It made her think about last night. About touching him last night. About the way he'd touched her. About the way he'd felt inside her.

She swallowed hard and fought to keep her expression breezy and natural.

Gabe glanced quickly over to the table, and on seeing that Ellie was focused on the book, he tilted his head so he could murmur in Lydia's ear. "You feel okay about... everything?"

She stiffened, worried that her discomfort had somehow been evident. "Why wouldn't I?"

"I don't know. I'm checking to make sure."

"I'm fine." She was overly conscious of his body, even covered in the sweatshirt. "Did you think I would swoon or something? I'm not a silly woman."

"I never said you were silly." His voice was just as soft, but now it sounded faintly annoyed. "I was just checking."

"Well, I could check with you about it too. Are you okay?" She was able to meet his eyes with a challenging look.

"I'm just fine too." His eyes had narrowed.

"Good."

"Good."

Now she was even more aware of his body. And his tension. And the reined-in passion she sensed beneath his reserve.

This was ridiculous. If he kept trapping her like this in the kitchen every morning, she was going to get turned on anytime she got close to a refrigerator.

"Are you guys fighting?" Ellie asked from the table, very

much as she'd asked the day before. She was still focused down on her book.

Gabe took a quick step back from Lydia. "Of course not." He turned back to his pancakes, which looked rather overdone.

"Were you kissing?" Ellie asked, glancing up now with a suspicious look.

"We're not fighting or kissing. We were just talking." He sounded casual, laid-back, but for some reason Lydia thought he might be uncomfortable.

"Are you keeping secrets?"

For no particular reason, Lydia felt a jolt of sympathy for Gabe, who looked like he was fighting to keep his patience and easy demeanor. So Lydia said lightly, "Maybe there's a reason for keeping secrets. It's not long until Christmas, you know."

Ellie looked over at her for the first time. "Oh."

Feeling vaguely pleased that she'd stymied the girl, Lydia poured herself some orange juice and then went to sit beside Ellie. "What are you reading?" she asked. "That's a really big book."

"I know," Ellie said soberly, showing Lydia the cover.

"Is it good?" Lydia studied the cover, having a faint recognition of the author but coming up with no piece of knowledge to add to the conversation about it. But she remembered as a girl that she'd always liked to talk about the books she was reading, so she asked, "Are they riding a Pegasus?"

"Yes."

"Is it good?"

"Yes."

"It's part of a series, isn't it? Is this the first one?"

"No. This is number four."

"Oh." Lydia was looking at the words on the pages now. It seemed pretty hard reading for such a little girl. "I wonder if I would like these books."

"Why would you like them?"

"Why wouldn't I? I like the Harry Potter books."

"You do?" Ellie's eyes widened.

"Yes, of course. Do you have the first of these books?"

"I have all of them. You can read them if you want."

Lydia felt a silly swell of pride that she was having an actual conversation with the girl, without even setting about with any sort of strategy. "Thank you. I can start the first one today."

Ellie nodded and accepted the plate of pancakes her dad set in front of her. "It's a good one."

Lydia glanced up when Gabe handed her a plate too, and she caught a strange look on his face. She wasn't sure what to make of it. A little bit questioning. A little bit cautious.

She had no idea what it meant.

But the pancakes were right there in front of her, so she ate them.

Lydia started Ellie's book that afternoon, and it was really a pretty good story. She actually was kind of sorry to put it down when she had to get ready for dinner at the church that evening.

Jessica and Alice had planned the dinner to celebrate

Lydia and Gabe's marriage. It was a potluck, so it was low-key, but Lydia still didn't much want to go.

Since it was in their honor, there was no way not to go though. She made an effort with her appearance and wore a nice pair of black pants and her favorite green dressy sweater.

On the way there, Lydia asked Ellie questions about the book. Ellie answered easily enough. She sounded faintly impatient, in that condescending little-girl way, but Lydia suspected she was pleased by the interest.

Gabe listened without saying much although Lydia caught him watching her more than once. He'd made an effort with his clothes too and wore a brown sport coat over his dress shirt.

Lydia was feeling strangely nervous as they got out of Gabe's car and entered one of the doors of the fellowship hall. She took a deep breath and reminded herself that there was nothing to be anxious or uncomfortable about.

They hadn't lied to anyone. They were married for real. People could be happy for them without it being some sort of deception.

Plus in a few months all of this would be over and she'd be in India where she'd wanted to be all this time.

She was ready to smile and greet people as they walked in. And then there was all the hassle of getting the dishes on the table and the line to fill their plates so there wasn't much time for more than small talk.

And then it all felt fine—like any of the innumerable church potlucks Lydia had been to in her life. Yes, there were flowers for her and a table full of cards—since she and Gabe had intentionally asked for no presents—but otherwise people acted normal.

Except Gabe was beside her the whole time.

He had his arm slung over the back of her chair as they were drinking coffee after the meal. Her brother Thomas was sitting across from them, and he and Gabe had been talking about football.

Lydia didn't mind football, but she couldn't seem to focus much on the conversation.

She was trying not to think about how much she liked the feel of Gabe's arm behind her.

In a lull in conversation, she glanced over and saw Ellie talking to Mia. She couldn't help but smile at the sight of Ellie obviously holding court and imparting some sort of nine-year-old wisdom to the younger girl.

"They seem to get along pretty well," she said, nodding toward the girls. "Even with the age difference."

"Mia is used to hanging out with adults," Thomas said, his face softening as he looked at his daughter.

He looked tired and faintly stressed, but he almost always looked that way.

"I'm glad she could come tonight," Lydia said.

"Me too. It's my weekend with her. She's been talking about the wedding for weeks now, so she was really excited to see you again to see if you looked any different."

Gabe chuckled, and Lydia smiled. "Why would I look different?"

Thomas gave a half shrug. "She seemed to think you might."

Honestly, Lydia felt different. If felt like so much had changed since she'd gotten married a couple of weeks ago.

But nothing really had changed at all. She was still her, and she was still going to India.

"So you have full custody of Ellie?" Thomas asked, looking over at Gabe.

The question was posed casually, and Gabe didn't seem annoyed by it. "Yes."

"Does her mother see her at all?"

Since his arm was around her, Lydia felt the slightest tension in his body. "Every once in a while. Very rarely. She... lives a different life."

Thomas nodded. He'd always been smart. He could tell he shouldn't go further into this conversation.

"How is Abigail?" Lydia asked softly. Since Thomas had brought up the conversation with Gabe, he couldn't complain that she'd asked herself.

And she'd always liked Thomas's wife. She'd been really upset when they'd separated.

Thomas looked at her, then glanced away. "She's doing fine."

"Has anything... changed?"

Her brother shook his head. "Nothing."

Lydia swallowed and leaned back against Gabe, who tightened his arm around her.

She didn't know exactly what had happened with her brother's marriage, but it was obviously something not easy to fix.

Jessica came over just then with a plate of lemon squares and sat down in an empty chair next to Thomas.

"Oh, I'm full—" Lydia began.

"Please, eat one," Jessica said with a wry grin. "Daniel

said I made too much, and if I have to take the whole plate home, he'll be proven right. You wouldn't do that to me, would you?"

Lydia laughed and accepted one although she really was pretty full. "Oh, it's good."

Jessica beamed. "No need to sound surprised."

Gabe took one too, eating his in three bites. When she saw a little powdered sugar on his jaw, she reached up without thinking to brush it off.

She kind of liked his expression as he gazed at her. It felt warm, intimate. Not at all what she was used to.

But when she turned back, everyone around was watching them with that silly, cheesy expression that made her cringe. Like they were all so pleased she was in love.

She wasn't in love. She was married to Gabe, but it was a purely practical arrangement.

He'd had sugar on his face, so she'd brushed it off for him. It was a decent thing to do. Not a sign that they were some sort of sappy, hackneyed couple.

She shifted away from Gabe slightly, and he dropped his arm.

She felt more herself on the way home, once all the intrusive eyes were no longer on them. Ellie had evidently had a really good time, and she was in a particularly happy mood. And Gabe was teasing her about the Christmas presents he'd bought for her, some that she would never guess.

Ellie tried to guess anyway, calling out increasingly extravagant possibilities. Lydia couldn't help but join in, guessing an apple tree, a ball gown, and a zebra, and causing Ellie to laugh hysterically at each one.

"Did you get me a... a... a new car?" Ellie shouted as they traipsed into the house. Her little face was beaming, and she was tugging on Lydia's sleeve in her excitement.

"Ooh, I want a new car too!" Lydia said, her voice rippling with laughter.

Gabe had kept his composure the whole time, but he was obviously enjoying himself. There was laughter in his eyes as he tried to give the two of them a smug look. "What if *I* want a new car for Christmas?"

"No, you have to get cars for us!" Ellie was clearly getting overly excited, and Lydia vaguely hoped there wouldn't be a crash soon. The girl ran over to Gabe, who swung her up in a hug.

"You won't even be able to drive it."

"But Miss... Aunt Lydia can drive mine and hers. Right?" Ellie looked over for confirmation.

"Right. I'm afraid we've left you no excuse." Just for fun, she went over to grab his shirt the way Ellie was.

She'd never seen Gabe look so relaxed, so happy. The warmth in his face and smile was intoxicating. No wonder Ellie was so giddy.

"I think I'm being ganged up on," he drawled. "And how will the cars fit under the tree?"

Ellie giggled at his comeback, but she was easily distracted. "When will we put up the Christmas tree, Daddy?"

"What about this weekend."

"Yay!" Ellie sprinted into the living room to find the right location for the tree.

"Bed in fifteen minutes," Gabe called, still smiling.

When he turned back to Lydia, she realized that she was still holding on to his shirt. And one of his hands had slid down to settle on her waist.

She felt a shiver of excitement, but it wasn't just physical. She just wanted to be close to him.

As close as she could get.

They stared at each other for a minute, and the feeling between them shifted, got hotter somehow.

Just last night, they'd had sex. They could have sex again tonight.

She wondered if he'd say something. If he'd come to her room.

He dropped his hand when Ellie came running back though, and Lydia silently told herself to get a grip.

She was still telling herself to get a grip when she changed clothes and went downstairs for a bottle of water.

She shouldn't be feeling this way. It wasn't what their marriage was about. And it would soon start to get in the way of what was most important.

Gabe's door was shut when she walked past it, but light was visible through the crack.

She suddenly realized that he would never come to her room. He'd told her from the beginning that sex was a standing offer, but it was clearly always going to be in her court.

If she wanted sex, she was going to have to ask for it.

If he'd made a move on her, she would have responded.

No problem. But she couldn't quite bring herself to knock on his door.

She wanted to. A lot. But maybe it would be better to use tonight to reorient herself to reality. To priorities.

Her life had always had clear priorities. A clear purpose.

And what was behind this door—maybe waiting right now to see if she would knock—just wasn't it.

CHAPTER 8

A FEW EVENINGS LATER, LYDIA WAS STANDING IN THE church fellowship hall again, watching the chaos around her.

It was the first joint rehearsal of the adult and children's choir for their songs at the Christmas Eve service, and it had slowly spiraled out of control.

It had started with everyone sitting quietly in seats, but that was an hour ago. Now the kids were running all over, and the adults were split into six or seven groups, conversing about everything from sports to children's costumes for the yearly pageant, which would be happening on this coming Sunday evening.

Jessica, who had been nominated as the organizer for the Christmas choir, was desperately trying to line the bigger kids up for their recitation of the nativity account in the Gospel of Luke.

Lydia had been annoyed at first since she liked things to run efficiently and quickly, but now she was closer to laughing.

Ellie was up with the bigger kids, waiting quietly in line as she'd been instructed. Since she was all by herself and Jessica was trying to round up the rest of the kids, Lydia walked over to stand next to the girl.

"Do you have your verse memorized?" she asked Ellie.

Ellie nodded. "Dad helped me with it this morning."

"Maybe you'll be able to practice if everyone will get in line." Glancing around, Lydia decided that, if more of the parents would help with crowd control, things would move smoother. Poor Jessica couldn't do it on her own.

"They're all crazy," Ellie said, observing the kids running around soberly. "I wish they would get in line."

"Come on now," Jessica said, more loudly than she was wont to speak. She was holding her rounded belly. "Everyone get in line so we can go through this one time!"

A few kids meandered over toward the line, but otherwise there was little effect—other than a few parents calling out for their kids.

Lydia met Jessica's gaze, and they shared a dry, resigned smile.

"I wish they would line up," Ellie said again.

She was starting to sound a little frustrated, and Lydia felt a wave of intense sympathy. She knew very well how it felt to want something to happen when people wouldn't cooperate. In response, she used her most resonant voice and boomed out, "Everyone age six to ten line up over here immediately!"

Her voice carried loudly all through the fellowship hall. There was an immediate silence in the aftermath and then a soft ripple of murmurs as the kids started to move into place.

Jessica laughed and mouthed, "Thank you," and Lydia felt a silly swell of pride at having accomplished such a feat.

Ellie moved closer to her and whispered, "That was really good."

Lydia grinned down at her, recognizing real appreciation on the girl's face for the first time.

Ellie actually smiled back and kind of pressed herself against her side.

Lydia put her arm around the girl with an unexpected wave of affection.

Without conscious thought, she glanced up and over to the far side of the hall where Gabe was working with a few other people who were constructing the backdrop of a stable for the pageant.

He was wearing jeans and a T-shirt, and he was looking over at her and Ellie at the moment. Their gaze met for a few seconds, and she had no idea how to understand the expression in his eyes.

But it made her feel even warmer, even deeper somehow.

It also made her feel rather uncomfortable, so she distracted herself by turning away and helping Jessica get the kids lined up in the right way.

It felt like Gabe might have still been watching her, but Lydia didn't glance over to check.

About a half hour later, the rehearsal had broken up after they'd rather sloppily gone through the entire program once.

Not everyone had left immediately, and some of the kids were running sprints back and forth across the fellowship hall as the remaining adults were putting the room back in order.

Lydia was helping to move chairs back around the tables so it would be ready for adult Sunday school. In the process of turning around with a chair in her hands, she jerked to a stop when she saw a toddler wobbling toward her.

Micah was right behind the little girl, and he scooped her up before she ran into Lydia.

"Sorry," he said, grinning in his warm, charismatic way. "Once she started to walk, she just won't stop."

"She gets around really well. She wasn't even walking at Easter." She smiled at the pretty, blue-eyed girl. "Hi, Cara. You look very pretty in that red sweater."

Cara hid her face in Micah's shirt.

"She's still really shy," he said, giving his daughter a little hug. "According to Alice, she needed some Christmas outfits, so we bought her all kinds of stuff."

"Oh, yeah." Lydia glanced over at Ellie, realizing that the girl would probably want something to wear for Christmas too. She hadn't even thought about it. "Gabe and I should look for something for Ellie, I guess."

"If he's like me, the idea might not even cross his mind."

She sighed. "It hadn't crossed my mind either."

"How are things going with Ellie?" Micah looked genuinely interested—and sympathetic in a way she appreciated.

"Okay. They're getting better. It's hard, you know, but she's a really sweet girl."

"You seem to be getting along really well."

"Really?" Lydia perked up at the thought that an outsider might have thought she wasn't a complete failure as a stepmother.

"Yeah. Don't you think so?"

"I don't know. I don't think I'm very good at it."

"It's probably harder because she's older, but she seems to like you okay."

Lydia felt even more optimistic. Maybe things were getting better than she'd realized. "I hope so." She glanced around, realizing she hadn't seen Micah's wife this evening. "Where is Alice?"

"She's working at the library this evening. They've finally been able to give her more hours."

"Oh. Good for her." Lydia smiled, remembering all the years when Micah had seemed so lonely and lost—even in the midst of his very active social life. She was so glad that he seemed to be happy now.

In response, she reached over to give Micah a friendly, one-armed hug.

"What was that for?" he asked, appearing genuinely curious.

"Nothing. Just that you did really well getting Alice."

He laughed. "You don't have to tell me that."

His eyes moved over her shoulder, and Lydia turned automatically to see what had distracted him. She jerked in surprise when she saw Gabe was standing right behind her.

She dropped her arm from around Micah and said, "Oh. Hi there. Are you ready to go?"

"Pretty soon." Gabe wasn't smiling—at her or at Micah. "Ellie is still playing."

Lydia saw the girl evidently trying to give instructions to two boys in arranging the chairs a certain way. She chuckled. "It looks like she's starting to make friends."

"Yes."

Gabe's voice seemed unnaturally cool, and he put his hand on her back as he stood beside her, moving her farther away from Micah without Lydia even really noticing it.

Lydia looked up at her husband in surprise, but he wasn't looking at her.

"How are you liking the house?" Micah asked, obviously trying to be friendly.

Gabe arched his eyebrows. "It's fine."

She frowned at him, afraid that Micah would think he was being rude. "We really like it," she told Micah. "It's wonderful."

She looked up at Gabe, hoping he'd add more to the conversation. He didn't though. He just watched Micah with a look that appeared almost challenging.

She was baffled by his mood, when he'd seemed in a perfectly fine mood earlier. And she hadn't seen anything happen this evening to justify such a decline.

Evidently sensing the conversation wasn't going anywhere, Micah said he needed to get Cara home to bed and said good-bye with another friendly grin.

Lydia told them good-bye, and Gabe just nodded.

With a frustrated inhale, Lydia turned to glare at him. "Why were you so rude?" she asked in a low voice.

"I'm not aware of doing or saying anything rude." Gabe was looking at her now, and he definitely wasn't happy.

Her lips parted. "You were all cold and off-putting.

Micah is a good guy, and he's going to think you don't like him."

"I'm sure my impressions are of no interest to him at all."

"What the hell, Gabe?" Her voice was still low so no one else would hear. "What's wrong with you?"

"Why do you assume something is wrong with me?"

"Because I know you, remember? This is not how you normally act. What happened? Did something happen? Micah is a good guy and a friend of mine, so I'd appreciate it if you'd at least be polite to him."

His eyes narrowed, and she felt a familiar tension radiating off him—the kind that told her he was angry. "You've now told me he's a good guy at least four times. Continually telling me isn't going to change my impression of him."

Lydia gaped, suddenly hit with a realization, an answer that explained almost everything about Gabe's strange mood. It was just such a ridiculous idea that she could barely process it.

"What?" Gabe demanded after a minute, his shoulders stiff and his gaze still cold.

"Are you jealous?" she whispered, leaning forward to speak even softer than she'd been before. "Are you jealous of *Micah*?"

"Why do you sound so surprised? You're my wife, for whatever reason we got married, and I don't think any husband would appreciate watching his wife embrace another man in front of the entire church."

She was almost choking on the shock and disbelief. "It was just friendly! Obviously, it was just friendly. We weren't embracing, and no one watching would have thought so—except for you. You must be crazy to think…" She trailed off, too surprised to even finish the thought.

"I must be crazy to think what?"

"That there's anything but friendliness between me and Micah." She put her hand on his chest and leaned toward him so she could speak into his ear, just to be sure no one else could hear. "Gabe, seriously. Micah is married. He's crazy in love with Alice. He's never had any real feelings for me even when we were dating in high school. And I have absolutely no feelings for him. How can you even think I would… I mean, I'm your wife. Don't you trust me at all?"

She got more and more upset as she continued until her voice cracked on the last words. He'd told her three months ago that he could never trust another woman with his heart, but it was only now that she was understanding what it meant.

It meant he might assume that she would cheat on him with the first man who passed by.

And it hurt. For some reason, it hurt a lot.

"Yes, I trust you," he murmured thickly. His mouth was about three inches from her face now. "I don't think anything is going on between you and Micah."

"But you just—"

"I don't think you are doing anything. Why should I assume you don't want to?"

They stared at each other for a tense moment, and she felt so emotional that she held on to his shoulders. "Because… because I don't," she whispered at last, telling him the truth—as she always did when she had no idea what to say. "I don't."

"You don't?"

"No. You're my husband. And that... means something to me."

As she said the words, she realized how true they were. No matter how practical and non-emotional their marriage, she had no interest in any other man. The idea of wanting someone else wasn't even on her radar anymore.

Evidently, the words got through to him because she saw his expression break for just a moment. "It means something to me too."

She suddenly realized that he felt the way she did. Maybe he'd just realized it too.

For a moment they seemed to completely understand each other.

She wasn't sure who moved first, but she ended up pressed tightly against him, his arms around her, holding her against him.

And it felt good. So good. Like he needed her, like he was offering strength and taking it both.

"I'm sorry," he murmured into her ear. "I know I need to work on trusting you."

"I hope you do," she said, pulling away. "I can see how it might be hard, but I hope you can. I'll do everything I can to live up to your trust. I hope you believe me."

He tightened his arms again. "I want to."

It was something. It was enough—at least for now. It made Lydia feel safer, warmer, closer to him than she'd ever been before.

When they finally pulled apart, Lydia felt strangely self-conscious, embarrassed in a way she rarely was. She noticed a few people were watching them, and she couldn't help but wonder what they thought had just happened between them.

Ellie was on her way over, her cheeks brightly flushed and her hair messy.

"Are you ready to head home?" Gabe asked, sounding natural again although he kept a hand on Lydia's back.

"Yes." Ellie looked from one of them to the other. "Are you fighting?"

"No. We were just hugging. You don't fight and hug at the same time, do you?"

Ellie narrowed her eyes in a look that was eerily like her father. "I don't know. You guys do."

Lydia couldn't help but smile. When the girl was right, she was right.

A few hours later Lydia hesitated in the hallway outside of Gabe's bedroom.

They hadn't had sex since the first time. She'd talked herself into thinking it would be simpler that way.

But she really wanted to spend the night with Gabe tonight. And not just because her body wanted it.

It felt strange though. To want it so much. She wasn't in the habit of acting on feeling. She'd been practical and reasonable all her life.

So she stood for a few minutes before she summoned up the will to make a move.

She really wasn't sure what the move was going to be until she saw herself knocking on his door.

She was breathless when the door swung open and

Gabe stood in front of her, wearing nothing but a pair of boxers.

"Sorry," she said. "Were you in bed?"

He just stared at her with those heavy-lidded eyes.

"It's fine if you'd rather not, but I was wondering if you want to... to—"

She was still getting the words out when he suddenly reached out for her and pulled her into a hard kiss.

Her mind thrilled with his obvious passion, and both her heart and her body reacted as he pulled her over to the bed, laid her down, kissed and caressed her into arousal, and then sank into her body.

She wrapped her arms around him and hung on as they started to move together rhythmically, both of them wordless, breathless. He wasn't quite as urgent this time, and her body was worked up into greater heights of pleasure, but she wasn't quite there when he fell out of rhythm and came with hoarse grunts of release.

She didn't have time to be disappointed since she loved the feel of his relaxed body on top of her. And then he started to kiss his way down her body until his mouth had settled between her legs.

It didn't take long for her to cry out as her body shuddered through a more intense orgasm than even last time.

He was smiling as he raised himself back up to the pillow, and she had to admit that she was smiling too.

"Thank you," she gasped, settling into the crook of the arm he wrapped around her. Her whole body was deliciously relaxed.

"What for?"

"Well, you did something really nice down there, you know."

He chuckled. She could feel it all through his body.

"I just mean I appreciate you making sure I got there too."

She wasn't looking at his face, but she could feel that he was still smiling. He brushed a kiss into her hair. "Evidently, when it comes to sex with you, patience is not my virtue, so I figure better late than never."

She giggled. "Definitely better late than never."

They lay together for a while, and Lydia found herself wondering what it would be like to share a room, a bed, with him. There was something nice about lying against him like this, even though the sex was over.

But soon they would be spending a large portion of the year apart, so she really needed to not get in the habit of it.

To distract herself from fuzzy thoughts, she murmured the first thing that entered her head. "It's kind of strange being married."

She felt him tilt his head to look at her face. "What do you mean?" He sounded almost wary.

Worried he'd misunderstood her random comment, she rushed through an explanation. "Nothing bad. I actually like it more than I thought. But it just feels kind of strange sometimes. I was thinking I wouldn't ever get married, and then here we are in bed together."

"What's wrong with that?" He still sounded confused, almost cautious, as if he were expecting her to say something that might hurt him.

She hated that feeling. Hated that he would even think that—when she was so far from wanting to hurt him.

"Nothing's wrong with it. I'm sorry if I'm saying this wrong. I have a bad habit of just saying what's in my head whether it makes sense or not."

He shifted a little so he was on his side and they could look each other in the eye in the darkened room. "It's not a bad habit. In fact, it's really... I want you to say what's on your mind. I'm just not sure what you mean."

She let out a relieved breath when she saw his expression was natural. "I don't know if I even mean anything, really. Just that I never would have expected to be here, like this. It's just not how I imagined my life. I guess a lot of women live waiting for this, but I never did. So now it's sometimes hard to wrap my head around it. But I like it. A lot." Realizing she'd rambled on and maybe said too much, she backpedaled a little. "I mean, it's better than I was thinking it would be. It's strange, but... but kind of good."

He smiled just a little. "It's better than I was thinking it would be too."

She let out another long exhale, relaxing as she realized she hadn't bumbled them into a misunderstanding. "Is it ever strange for you too?"

He gave a little shrug. "Yeah, I guess it is. I was thinking I'd never get married again, so sometimes I wake up and go through this moment of realization as I remember I'm not alone—I mean, as I remember I'm married."

"I do that too. And I guess maybe it's even stranger for you since you were married before."

"I don't know." His eyes were sober even in the dark. "Being with you is completely different from being with Michaela."

He didn't talk about his ex-wife much, so Lydia's breath caught in her throat. She murmured, "In what way?"

"In every way. Being with you feels different in every way. It's a different kind of marriage—and it was from the very beginning."

Of course it was, Lydia realized. He'd been in love with Michaela, and he wasn't in love with her. Naturally, it would feel completely different. She felt irrationally deflated, but she fought against the feeling. It was silly to dwell on things like that.

"But I think it's working out pretty well," she said, holding on to the hope she'd been feeling earlier. "I think we can really make this work."

"I think so too."

She smiled at him. "And I'll try not to blurt out random things I think about."

He chuckled and reached out to stroke her hair back from her face in an oddly tender gesture. "No, I don't want you to hold things back."

"You have no idea what you're asking for," she said, her voice tinged with laughter. "I think a lot of crazy, random things."

"Well, go ahead and tell me them. I want to know what you're thinking and feeling. I never knew… with Michaela. I didn't know what she was…"

Lydia's breath caught again, and the laughter dissipated immediately as she realized he was trying to say something hard. She prompted as gently as she could, "You didn't know what she was thinking?"

"No. I had no idea. She acted like everything was

perfectly fine in our marriage, right up to the day she walked out the door."

Lydia froze for a moment, trying to process the words that still lingered in the silent air between them. "You never fought or anything?" she asked at last.

"We never fought. Ever. I'm not saying I did everything right. I made plenty of mistakes. And maybe I should have realized how unhappy she was becoming. But I didn't know. I didn't see it. She never told me. She put on this mask of being a content wife and mother, and I believed it. And then I was blindsided when she walked out. And sometimes I'm..." He trailed off, his voice rough with emotion.

"You're what?"

"Sometimes I'm scared it's going to happen again."

Lydia sucked in a sharp breath. "It's not. Gabe, I'm committed to this marriage. I thought you knew—"

"I do know. But things happen anyway."

"I know they do. But I'll tell you if I'm unhappy. I promise I will. I've always basically said what I thought, and I pretty much suck at hiding my feelings anyway."

He was almost smiling again. "I'm glad. That you suck at hiding your feelings, I mean."

She giggled, feeling better, like they were really understanding each other. "I guess that's why you're always asking me if everything is okay."

"I didn't realize I did that, but yes, it probably is. If something is worrying you, I want you to tell me."

"I will. I'll tell you. But I'm pretty sure that, if something is really bothering me, you'll know."

His smile broadened, and he pulled her back against

him so she was pressed up against his side, his arm surrounding her.

And she felt good. Really good. Really close to him.

Like this marriage was more than it really was.

She wasn't going to lie to him, but she also wasn't going to lie to herself. So after several minutes, she stretched against him and pressed a soft kiss on his jaw. "I'm going to bed, I guess."

Better not start to indulge in silly thoughts if she could possibly help it. And distance seemed wiser at the moment.

"You don't have to," he said, loosening his arm with what felt like reluctance.

"Thank you. But I think I will."

She went back to her room and went to bed alone, still wishing she didn't have to.

CHAPTER 9

A week later, Lydia was hiding a smile at the way Gabe looked as he waited for his coffee to brew on a Friday morning.

His hair was sticking straight up on end, and his T-shirt was on inside-out. He desperately needed to shave, and he was glaring at the one-cup brewer as if he could will the coffee to stream into the cup faster.

She'd gone to his room every night for a week except last night, when she'd started to worry about how hard it was to leave and go to her own room after they'd had sex. She was starting to feel too dependent, less in control than she was used to, so she'd stayed in her own room last night.

She hadn't slept very well, and it didn't look like Gabe had either, if his grumpy expression was anything to go by.

But unlike her, Gabe was kind of cute when he was in a grouchy mood.

"What are you laughing at?" he muttered without even turning to look at her.

"I'm not laughing." They'd gotten up at roughly the

131

same time, so she was now leaning against the counter, waiting for her turn with the coffeepot. "What are you talking about?"

He turned to check her face. "It feels like you're laughing."

"What happened to your hair last night?" she asked, feeling oddly tender. Without thinking, she stepped over and reached up to smooth down his hair. It just sprang back up when she pulled away her hand.

"Your hair doesn't look entirely neat itself." As if in retaliation, he reached over to touch her messy hair, but there was a new warmth in his eyes that she liked.

"Well, mine is at least responding to gravity." She was smiling up at him now as he stepped in toward her, trapping her against the counter. "Why are you in a bad mood this morning?"

"I'm not in a bad mood." He'd planted his hands on the edge of the counter on either side of her.

"Well, you were until I laughed at your hair." She was getting a little breathless at his proximity. She'd lain in bed a long time last night, thinking about him. She hadn't really thought that sex would ever be a major part of her life, but her body was definitely getting used to it and didn't appreciate the fast from it last night.

He leaned in even closer. "You said you weren't laughing."

"Maybe I was laughing a little."

"Why didn't you come to my room last night?" His voice was low and thick, and his eyes took on that sultry look she loved.

Her breath hitched. "I... don't know. Were you waiting for me?"

"I thought you might come."

"You could have come to my room, you know."

"What do you mean?"

"I mean, you're allowed to initiate if you want." Her body was shivering now, and she was starting to wonder if it was appropriate to have sex at six fifteen in the morning—from time to time.

"I didn't want to apply any undue pressure," he murmured, his lips glancing briefly against hers.

Her body was responding quickly to the tension she sensed in his and to the heat in his eyes, but she managed to arch her eyebrows. "And what exactly constitutes undue pressure?"

"Maybe me showing up in your bedroom at night with a raging hard-on."

She choked on a burst of amusement and wrapped her arms around him. She'd had no idea three months ago that he was so funny and smart and surprisingly sensitive.

He was a very good husband to have.

And maybe it didn't really matter that she was growing accustomed to having sex with him, being with him in other ways too. He was her husband, after all, and this marriage was working out a lot better than she'd ever imagined.

"So should I come to your room tonight?" he asked, brushing his lips against hers again. He tasted faintly like coffee.

"If you want to."

"I want you to want it too."

"If I don't want it, I'll send you away." She couldn't seem to stop smiling.

For the first time that morning, his lips turned up in an answering smile as he kissed her. When she tightened her arms around him, the kiss grew deeper. She arched her body into his as she was swept with waves of pleasure—more emotional than physical now.

He made a soft, husky noise in his throat when they were jarred from the embrace by a voice coming from the entrance to the kitchen. "Dad."

Both of them jerked, and Gabe turned his head abruptly, still imprisoning Lydia with his arms. "Good morning, Ellie," he said after a moment of orienting himself.

"What are you doing?"

What they were doing should have been self-evident, but Lydia figured the question was more an accusation that a genuine inquiry. Ellie didn't look happy at all as she stood, fully dressed and with her hair in a ponytail, glaring at them.

"We were talking," Gabe said, managing to sound mostly natural. "You're up early."

"I woke up."

"Are you ready for breakfast?"

"Yes, please."

"Okay." Gabe turned back to Lydia, a faint wryness in his expression, causing her to smile in response. He'd been getting into the kiss but not so much that it was a real problem for him to pull away from her body. "Do you want eggs or cereal?"

"Cereal, please."

While he went over to the cupboard, Lydia stuck her cup under the coffeemaker and hit the brew button. "What do you want to do today, Ellie?" she asked.

"I want to go Christmas shopping."

"Oh, that would be fun. I've got to do some shopping too. I can take you if you want."

"I want Dad to take me."

"I can't, pumpkin. I have a lot of work I need to do today." Gabe had returned to his coffee and emptied half of it in three long gulps, the box of cereal in his hand.

Ellie frowned. "But I wanted to go shopping with you."

"You can go with Aunt Lydia instead."

"We can go to that big bookstore in Dalton if you want. We can find some good presents there." Lydia tried to make her voice sound bright. She'd been getting along better with the girl for the past week, but she was still pretty sure Ellie would be just as happy not to have her around.

Ellie sighed. "Okay."

Gabe walked over and ruffled his daughter's hair. "Well, you don't need to sound so excited about it. If you don't want to go happily, then you can stay at home and not go at all."

The girl's face adjusted, as if she'd realized that her disapproval wasn't going to get her dad to change his mind. "No, I'll go."

"What do you say?"

"Thank you," Ellie said, looking up at Lydia.

Lydia sighed. "You're welcome." She was actually happy to take the girl shopping since she felt more comfortable around her now than she used to. But she hated the feeling that she'd somehow gotten the girl in trouble with her dad.

It still kind of felt like they were a family, and she was just hanging out with them.

And that feeling bothered her a lot more than it used to.

The shopping trip actually went well. Once Ellie was in the car, she perked up, and they spent the forty-minute drive talking about the book series that Lydia was now almost through reading.

They went to the bookstore first and spent an hour looking through the children's section and then another half hour having hot chocolate and cinnamon rolls in the attached café.

They went to the mall afterward and visited a big department store and a kids' clothes boutique, looking for a couple of cute Christmas sweaters for Ellie and a pretty Christmas dress for her to wear.

Everything went well until Ellie decided that she wanted to buy her dad a tie with books on it.

It all went downhill from there.

It was late in the afternoon before they finally got home. Ellie was crying, and Lydia was nearly in tears herself.

"Look," she said softly, hoping to calm Ellie down before Gabe emerged from his office. She held her phone down to Ellie. "I found this really nice tie with books on it online, and we can order it and have it here in two days. Isn't this what you were looking for?"

Lydia knew it was what the girl had been looking for, but just like before it didn't seem to satisfy her. Her cheeks streamed with tears. "I said we should keep looking."

"We'd looked at every store in the mall, and I called the rest of them in the county. We wouldn't have been able to find it." Her voice cracked—since she was both frustrated and upset. "Let me just order this for you and—"

"No," Ellie interrupted with a scowl. "I don't want it."

"Ellie." Gabe's voice snapped from down the hall. "You know better than to talk that way."

The girl jerked, obviously taken aback by her dad's presence.

Lydia, on the other hand, felt a deep wave of relief.

"Go up to your room. I'll be there in a few minutes." Gabe looked at her sternly.

Ellie ducked her head and ran upstairs with a little whimper.

Lydia smothered a groan and dropped the shopping bags on the floor.

"What happened?" Gabe asked, stepping closer to her.

"I don't even know. She wanted a certain tie for you for Christmas, and they just didn't have it at any stores at the mall. She got so upset about it. I wasn't sure what to do."

Gabe's eyebrows drew together, and he put an arm around her. Lydia slumped against him gratefully, feeling a little guilty for wanting his support so much but not about to turn it down.

"Are you okay?" he murmured, stroking her hair.

She exhaled, her cheek against his shoulder. "Yeah, I'm fine. It's just upsetting when she was so upset and nothing I did seemed to help."

"I don't know why she was so upset about something like that. She doesn't usually make a big deal about such little things. Was she talking to you the whole time the way I heard just now?"

Lydia was relaxing, feeling better, responding to his warmth and his strength. "It wasn't that big a deal."

"Lydia." There was a warning in his voice, and he raised her head to meet her eyes. "Tell me the truth."

"She was really upset. She wasn't thinking about how she was talking. Don't be too hard on her."

"I'm not going to be too hard on her, but I can't let her behave that way."

"I know. But she's had a rough time." Lydia dropped her eyes briefly, feeling uncharacteristically self-conscious. "With the marriage and all. She's had a rough time."

Gabe's expression changed. "Has she been behaving this way with you before?"

Lydia shook her head. "No. Not like this. She hasn't… I mean, she's been having trouble adjusting, but it's normal. I need to be patient. I know I need to be patient."

"What do you need to be patient about? Why the hell didn't you tell me you'd been having trouble with her? You said you would tell me if you were unhappy about anything. You said you would tell me the truth."

He looked hurt as well as annoyed, and Lydia felt suddenly guilty. He was right. She should have told him. She'd been keeping it from him, and that was just wrong. However small, it was a betrayal of his trust.

"I know," she said, her voice cracking. "I'm sorry. But I haven't been unhappy. It's really not that big a deal."

"But you've been having trouble with her."

"I haven't. I mean, we've been doing as well as can be expected. I'm certainly not going to go whining to you about not getting enough warm fuzzies. It's getting better. She's a good kid, and it's getting better."

"Damn it, Lydia." He turned his head, breathing heavily, obviously thinking. "I wish you would have told me. I could have helped."

"How, exactly?"

"I could have talked to Ellie."

"And then she might have acted differently but not felt differently. We can't force her to like me, Gabe. It's going to take time."

"I thought she *was* liking you. I thought…" He drifted off, looking away from her again. He felt strangely vulnerable in a way she just wasn't used to.

"I think she likes me more now than she did. I'm trying to be patient." She gave Gabe a ghost of a smile, wanting him to be himself again. "You know how hard that is for me."

He returned her smile with a tilt of his lips. "I do."

"I'm sorry I didn't tell you. I shouldn't have held it back. At first I just didn't want to complain, and then I didn't want you to worry. But I should have told you. I'm really sorry."

"It's okay." He leaned over and brushed a kiss against her lips. "Thank you. For making such an effort with her."

"It's fine," Lydia said, flushing with pleasure. "I want to. I lo—"

"You what?" he asked, almost urgently, when she broke off her instinctive word.

"I… I don't know. I was uncomfortable with her at first

but now… now I kind of love her." Admitting such a thing was more embarrassing than she could remember feeling. But she realized it was true. It was growing, but it was true.

Gabe made a rough sound in his throat and pulled her into a hard hug. Lydia clung to him, feeling closer to him than she could ever remember feeling to anyone except her family.

She was reveling in the feeling when Gabe abruptly pulled away. He wasn't looking in her eyes, and he seemed strangely stiff for no reason that made any sense. "What kind of tie was she looking for?"

"One with something on it she wanted special for you." Lydia wasn't about to break the girl's confidence. "I found one online that would be perfect, but she was upset that she couldn't find it in the store. We looked in every single store, and then I called up all the others in the county." She shook her head, thinking about how hard she'd tried to find the tie for Ellie.

They found striped ties and checked ties and polka-dotted ties and tacky Christmas ties, and ties with golf clubs and race cars and fishing poles on them. But no books.

"Okay. I'll go talk to her."

"Be gentle. She's having a really hard time." Lydia felt strangely like she'd lost something. He seemed changed since they'd been hugging just a moment before, and she didn't know why.

"She still needs to be behave."

"I know."

"Actually, why don't you come up too?"

Lydia blinked since it had always been understood that

any disciplining or decision-making regarding Ellie would be done by Gabe. "What? Why?"

"To help." He looked strangely awkward, and he glanced over his shoulder toward the stairs. "I think you should be part of it too."

So for no good reason, Lydia's heart began to race almost painfully. "You want me to..."

"I think we should do it together."

She had no idea how she was feeling or why she was feeling anything so intense to such a minor incident, but she was having trouble taking a full breath. "Okay. I'll be up in just a minute."

She wasn't actually sure whether she'd be up or not. She was irrationally terrified.

Gabe was already heading up the stairs, so there was no sense in staring up at his strong back and fine ass.

She wondered how hard it had been for him all these years to raise Ellie all on his own.

She did want to help him. She wanted to be part of both Gabe's and Ellie's lives. She wanted to be part of his family. She wanted it so much it ached in her chest.

But going upstairs right now to work through things with Ellie—like a family, as a family—would mean that everything would change.

It would mean that this marriage was a lot more than a means to the end she wanted.

She went to the bathroom and got some water from the kitchen. Then she called her mom to kill some time. She didn't tell her mother about what happened, but her mom obviously realized something was wrong.

When Lydia left one too many comments unanswered, her mother asked softly, "What's wrong, honey?"

"I... really don't know."

"You sound upset."

"I'm not. Not really. I'm just..." Lydia really had no idea what she was.

After a moment, her mom replied, "Well, whatever it is, I know you'll face it head on. You've always been the bravest person I know."

Lydia made a choked sound of appreciation. "Thanks, Mom. I've got to go, but I'll talk to you tomorrow."

After they said good-bye, Lydia grabbed the shopping bags and hauled them upstairs, putting some of the stuff in her room before heading up to the third floor to Ellie's garret room.

She should have come up with him from the beginning. She wanted to make sure the girl was okay. And Gabe was okay too.

She listened briefly at the door before she tapped on it. When Ellie called out to come in, Lydia brought the bags with Ellie's books and clothes into the room. "I'm just bringing up your stuff. Is everything okay?"

Ellie and Gabe were propped up against the headboard, Gabe's arm around the girl. Ellie had obviously been crying, but she wasn't now. "Yeah, everything's okay."

Lydia darted her eyes over to Gabe, who gave a little nod. So Lydia smiled as she draped the red velvet Christmas dress over the chair and then came over to the bed.

"I'm sorry I was mean to you," Ellie said as Lydia sat down on the edge of the bed.

"Thank you. I know it was upsetting."

"I didn't mean to make you feel like I didn't appreciate you."

Those words sounded like Gabe, but they seemed sincere enough coming from the girl with her earnest blue eyes.

Lydia nodded, touched by the sentiment. "I thought we had a good time until the end."

"We did. Thank you for taking me."

"You're welcome. I'm glad we were able to go. And did you want me to order..." Instead of finishing the sentence, Lydia gestured down toward her phone.

Ellie nodded soberly. "Yes, please."

Lydia exhaled in relief, and Gabe leaned down to press a kiss into Ellie's hair.

She wasn't really great at this—at kids or marriage or anything—but Lydia decided she was doing all right.

They ordered pizza for dinner, and they ate it in the living room as they watched two Christmas movies in a row— one animated and one old classic musical.

Ellie started on the floor, while Gabe and Lydia sat on the couch. By the time the second movie started, however, all three of them were on the couch, Lydia leaning against Gabe on one side and Ellie leaning against him on the other.

Gabe seemed perfectly comfortable, so Lydia couldn't quite bring herself to pull away even though she felt a brief nervousness churning in her gut when she realized she was enjoying the evening a lot.

A lot.

And this wasn't going to last. Everything would change when she got to India.

She drowned out that thought and relaxed instead.

Ellie was asleep at the end of the second movie, and Gabe was gently stroking Lydia's hair. It felt tender, like he cared for her, like he wanted to protect her. It just intensified the soft feelings that were starting to overwhelm her.

When the movie ended, Lydia straightened up a little so she could look at him. They stared at each other for a minute, their faces only two inches apart.

Then she saw his face change, and she knew he was going to kiss her in the moment before he did.

The kiss wasn't passionate or particularly urgent, but it was lingering. It didn't end right away. She leaned into him as their lips brushed against each other, his tongue gently slipping out to stroke the insides of her lips.

"Baby," he murmured.

"Hmm." She didn't pull away. In fact, she reached up to tangle her fingers in his thick hair. He'd never called her that before, but it felt natural, made her feel even softer.

"Are you okay with everything?"

Her head was spinning a little with feeling, so she couldn't quite follow the question. "Hmm?"

He leaned forward to kiss her again, one hand cupping her face. "Are you okay with how things are? Between us?" He was speaking very softly although Ellie was sound asleep.

"Of course." She was so surprised that she pulled back a little. "Why wouldn't I be?"

"I don't know. I just wanted to make sure."

"I'm good." She met his gaze, trying to read how he was feeling in the heavy-lidded blue eyes. "Aren't you?"

"Yeah. Yeah, of course. But I still think this marriage might be giving me more than it does you."

"No." She shook her head, realizing what he was worried about. "It's been good for me. Really good."

He smiled, and he was still smiling when he kissed her again.

Lydia was feeling more emotional than aroused, but the feelings were just as powerful. She'd never known she was capable of feeling this way. And it thrilled her and terrified her both.

They were still kissing when Ellie shifted on the couch, reminding them that they weren't alone. "Daddy."

"I'm here, sweetheart. You better get to bed."

Ellie roused herself enough to get up, and Gabe gestured to Lydia in a silent request to come up with them to put Ellie to bed. She'd never done that before, but she didn't hesitate. They both went up to say prayers with Ellie and kiss her goodnight.

When they came down, Lydia felt too full and a little self-conscious, so she picked up the pizza boxes and water bottles and straightened up the kitchen a little while Gabe went to return a call.

She went to her bedroom and decided that, since it had been a long day, she would feel better if she took a shower.

She was definitely going to be visiting Gabe's bedroom. Soon.

After she got out of the shower, she was wishing she had something sexy to wear. She didn't have anything sexy in her entire wardrobe. She had some pretty underwear, but all of her sleepwear was bought for comfort.

She pulled on a pair of panties and a pale blue tank top, searching her drawer for something other than the flannel pants she normally slept in.

Maybe a miracle would occur and something sexy would materialize that she'd forgotten about.

No such luck.

She jerked in surprise when she heard a knock on her door. She froze for a moment, processing the fact that the only person it could be was Gabe.

"Lydia?" his low voice came from outside the door.

She ran over and opened it. "Hi," she said, taking in the fact that he wore his normal sleepwear of pajama pants and T-shirt.

He gave her a little smile. "Hi."

She stared at him, feeling a wash of pleasure that he obviously wanted her so much tonight that he'd broken his habit of waiting for her to initiate.

"Can I come in?" he asked, glancing down and then back up again. "Or you could come to my room if you'd rather."

"You can come in." She stepped out of the way, telling herself to get a grip and not be so ridiculously happy about such a little thing.

He looked slightly self-conscious and evidently misread her silence. "You said I could initiate. But if you don't feel like it, then that's totally f—"

"No," she interrupted. "I do feel like it. I was planning to come to your room, but I wanted to take a shower first."

She looked down at herself, realizing she still just wore her tank and underwear. He'd obviously seen her without clothes before, but it felt different in her own bedroom, with the lights on.

He was looking at her body too.

"I was trying to find pajamas," she explained, gesturing toward the open drawer with a couple of pants hanging over.

"I really don't think you need to bother." His voice was huskier than normal.

She laughed and gestured toward the bed. "I might get cold tonight if I don't have pants to put on. But you can get in bed. Unless you'd prefer your room."

"Doesn't matter to me."

She went to grab a pair of flannel pants and matching top from the drawer, to put on if she got cold later. Then she headed toward her bed where Gabe was pulling down the covers and stretching out.

He looked as handsome and masculine as ever, but he also looked kind of rumpled, kind of tired. Human in a way that somehow surprised her.

This incredible man, lying on her bed. Still just a regular person.

And her husband.

"What?" he asked, evidently seeing something in her expression.

"Nothing." Her eyes darted down unconsciously, and she noticed something. "Are you turned on already?" she asked, genuinely surprised.

He frowned at her haughtily. "Is that a problem?"

"No. It just seemed fast."

"Well, you're the one standing there wearing almost nothing. What would you expect?"

She glanced down at herself. While nothing looked particularly special about her body—just her normal long legs, toned muscles, decent but not terribly impressive breasts—she suddenly realized that he really liked how she looked.

Really liked it, if the evidence of his arousal was anything to go by.

Maybe it was silly, but it thrilled her.

"Ever since I've married you," she admitted, trying to be as honest as she'd always been, "I've never known what to expect."

He smiled as she came over to him, and he said as she crawled onto the bed, "You don't think I'm some sort of a perv, do you?"

She'd been moving over him, unable to resist the sight of him, but she paused at the unanticipated question. "Perv? What does that mean?"

He reached over to pull her all the way over him so she was straddling his hips. "I mean, you were my babysitter once. You don't think I'm some sort of perv for getting so turned on by you now."

The words—and the feeling underlying it—sent another shiver of pleasure through her body. She slid her hands from his belly and up to his chest, over his shirt. "You weren't having lascivious thoughts about me back then, were you?"

"Of course not!"

He sounded so offended that she giggled and leaned down to kiss him. "Then you're fine. That was a long time ago."

His hands cupped her bottom, settling her down on top of him so that she could feel his erection through the fabric. "I guess so."

"And I'm your wife," she added, feeling her own body start to respond. "You're allowed to get turned on by me."

"Well, that's a relief." He was chuckling as she kissed him, but he soon took over the kiss, taking her head in one hand and sliding his tongue into her mouth.

She was breathless when they finally pulled apart, and she shifted her hips restlessly, arousal pulsing between her legs. "And you're allowed to do something about it," she added throatily.

He made a guttural sound and pulled her top off over her head, staring at her naked breasts hungrily. "Lucky me."

She rubbed herself against his erection. "I might be a little lucky myself."

He stroked her body skillfully, from her thighs to her hips and up to her breasts. She arched her back into his touch, still straddling his lap, and she gasped in pleasure as he twirled her nipples.

"Do you like that?" he asked, although he must already know the answer.

"Fuck," she gasped, arching even more as he sustained the caress. It was the first time she'd ever said the word as an exclamation, but it somehow came out of her mouth uninvited. "It feels so good."

"It looks like it feels good."

She probably looked shamelessly eager, starting to rock

as the pulsing of arousal grew too strong for her to control, but she just couldn't care. His hands stroked her, and his body was hot and hard beneath her. He could give her body exactly what she needed.

Her gasps turned to whimpers and then to moans as one of his hands slid down her belly and even lower.

Her body jerked when his fingers found her clit. "That seems like it might be a good spot," he murmured, a smile in his voice.

Her eyes had fallen closed as the pleasure intensified, and she reached back to cling desperately to his thighs to keep her balance. "It is," she panted. "Oh, it is. Please make me come."

"I'm definitely going to make you come. I want to see you totally come apart for me."

She was already on the verge of coming apart, and more so as his erotic voice worked her into higher tension. She was shaking now, trying to grind herself against him as he massaged her clit and squeezed her bottom with his other hand.

"I love how responsive you are," he murmured, his voice another caress. "I love how easily I can turn you on."

She'd never in her life liked to think she was easy, but there was no denying how quickly he could arouse her. She was close to orgasm already, panting desperately and making a lot of silly, helpless sounds.

Two of his fingers suddenly slid inside her channel as his thumb kept pressing into her clit. The sudden penetration pushed her over the edge, and she bent back like a bow as the waves of pleasure slammed into her.

She bit her lip to stifle her cry of release as she shuddered through the contractions, her inner muscles squeezing around his fingers.

He was stroking her gently when she'd finally worked through all the spasms, her body washed with delicious satisfaction. "Wow," she sighed, her voice cracking on the word. "That was..." She slumped over him, trying to get her mind to work when it was doing nothing but howling about how good her body felt at the moment.

"That was what?" he asked, stroking her back and still holding her bottom with one hand.

"That was... beyond words."

"Well, good." He tilted his head to kiss her hair. "I love how you're not at all self-conscious."

For the first time, a ripple of self-consciousness ran through her. Maybe he thought it was strange that she wasn't more shy or reticent about sex since she had only a couple of weeks' experience. "Is that strange?"

"I don't know what's strange." He met her eyes when she lifted her head. "I've only had sex with two women in my whole life, so I have no measure of what's normal. I'm just saying that I really like that about you."

"Okay. Good." He seemed to mean it, so she decided there was nothing to worry about.

She felt so relaxed she didn't really want to move, but she could feel the bulge of his erection beneath her, reminding her that there was more to come.

He'd made her feel so good, and she could make him feel really good too.

That thought inspired her enough to raise up again and adjust enough so she could slide down his pants. She took his erection into her hands as it was freed, and she loved the way he inhaled sharply in response to her touch.

She leaned down to kiss him as she stroked him, and soon he was lining her up above him again, moving aside her panties, and aligning his erection at her entrance.

She sank down over him, gasping at the tight penetration. Then she started to move over him as best she could, going by instinct since she'd never been on top before. She held Gabe's eyes as she moved, and it seemed to make the whole thing hotter.

He rocked his hips to match her motion, and he held on to her bottom, keeping their alignment snug. "Yes, baby. So good. Keep moving just like that."

Encouraged, she tried to keep an even rhythm, but everything was feeling so good that she kept getting excited and moving faster. Gabe was groaning in pleasure as she tried to rein in her instinct to grind against him.

They were gazing into each other's eyes as the pleasure built up between them. And they were still gazing into each other's eyes as she lost control and started to bounce shamelessly as another, deeper orgasm tightened inside her. And they were still gazing into each other's eyes when he choked on a desperate sound.

She was almost sobbing, trying to reach that elusive peak. "Gonna come," she gasped, to let him know she was close, in case he couldn't tell.

"I know, baby." His features twisted in effort, and he moved a hand between their bodies to fumble near where they were joined.

Despite her frantic motion, he found what he was looking for and gave her clit a clumsy massage.

She cried out as an orgasm hit her, freezing for a moment before letting go.

"That's right," Gabe murmured throatily as she shook desperately. "Ride it out, baby. Take everything you want. Don't hold anything back."

She rode him hard, sustaining the pleasure for so long she was hoarse when the pleasure finally faded. But it wasn't over yet because Gabe had finally let go himself.

She watched his face break with the climax, felt his body rock hard as he came beneath her, heard him choking out a helpless sound as if he couldn't hold anything back either.

She collapsed on top of him afterward, and he gathered her in his arms. And she loved how hot his body was, how it was starting to soften.

It felt as good as her own body felt—like he'd needed and taken as much as she had.

"Baby," Gabe was still murmuring with his gasps.

And she loved that too.

She had no idea how long they lay together, neither of them able to talk. Then she finally started to feel the chill of the room and rolled off him so she could reach down for her pajamas.

They smiled at each other as Lydia pulled up the covers and Gabe reached over to turn off the light. He reached out for her, and she snuggled against him.

It was a long time before she realized that he wasn't going to go back to his room for the night.

CHAPTER 10

LYDIA OPENED HER EYES THE NEXT MORNING TO DISCOVER that Gabe was still in bed with her. It was the first time in her life she'd ever woken up with a man.

She felt strange and groggy and soft, and it took a minute for her to register that Gabe was still asleep. It must be morning since light was streaming in through the edges of the blinds, and she could clearly see his closed eyelids, his dark eyelashes, the stubble on his jaw, the hair on the arm that was resting over the covers.

He was breathing slowly, deeply. Occasionally making a slight noise. She watched him for a while until she wondered if it was creepy to watch a guy while he slept.

She was working through this enigma in her mind when Gabe started to shift. She was watching as there was a momentary break in his breathing and then his eyes opened.

He turned his head and blinked at her.

"Hi," she said since she couldn't think of anything else to say.

A smile spread slowly over his face. "Hi." He rolled over on his side so he was facing her.

She opened her mouth to say something but couldn't come up with anything intelligent. Babbling out how she was feeling—that she was really glad he was in her bed, really glad he was her husband—might be too much for first thing in the morning.

"I thought this bed didn't feel quite right," he said, stretching out his legs under the covers.

"What's wrong with my bed?"

"Nothing. It's just softer than mine. And smaller." His smile broadened, and his eyes took on that intimate warmth she loved. "Kind of like you."

She snorted. "I'm not exactly small, you know."

"You're smaller than me."

"And soft isn't a word that most people apply to me."

"What do they know?" He reached over and pulled her against him. "I'm your husband, and I say you're softer and smaller than me."

She giggled and wrapped her arms around him. "I guess I can give you that much."

"I'll take anything you give me," he murmured against her hair, moving her body so she was pressed up fully against him.

She felt relaxed and content and like she wanted to keep touching him—but not particularly urgent. He seemed to feel the same way since he didn't try to deepen their embrace. So she just enjoyed the feel of lying in his arms like this. Not about sex. Just about being together.

Maybe this was what it was like to have a husband for real.

"I should get up," Gabe said, still sounding sleepy, without all of his normal edges.

"It's not even eight yet." She didn't feel like getting up, and she didn't want him to get up either. She stroked his chest over his T-shirt.

"Yeah. I don't normally sleep this late."

"Me either."

"I've got to drive to Raleigh today, so I need to leave by nine thirty or so."

She stiffened since this was the first time she was hearing about this. "What? Why?"

"It's just a lunch meeting. We arranged it late yesterday afternoon, and I forgot about it when you and Ellie came home. I'm coming back this afternoon." He shifted slightly. "Is that okay?"

"Of course. It's fine. I thought you meant you'd be out of town for a while."

"My folks said they'd watch Ellie today, so I wasn't trying to pressure you into watch—"

"I know. I don't mind that. I'm happy for Ellie to stay with me since I don't have anything going on today anyway. I just thought you meant you were going to be gone for a while." She realized she was repeating herself, but she felt compelled to explain her reaction.

When he didn't answer, she looked up at his face to see that he was smiling—just a little.

"What?" she demanded.

He shook his head. "Nothing. It just seems like maybe you would have missed me if I left."

She felt her cheeks reddening, which was ridiculous since she never blushed. "Why would I have missed you?"

He leaned down to brush her lips gently with his. "I have no idea."

"Well, don't get smug about it. I bet you'll miss me when I go visit churches through South Carolina, Georgia, and Alabama after Christmas."

"What?" He frowned. "When is this?"

"In January or February. I don't have it scheduled yet, but that's what I was planning—to get some more churches on board with my work in India. I'll probably be gone for a couple of weeks." She felt a little thrill at his disapproving expression. "So I bet you'll miss me then."

"Why didn't you tell me about this?"

He sounded more than teasingly disapproving. He sounded faintly annoyed.

She sat up on the bed. "I didn't have it planned yet. I was just in the early stages. Of course I'd talk to you about the schedule and everything."

"Oh."

"Is something wrong? You don't have a problem with me doing something like that, do you? I mean, you know the work I want to—"

"Of course I know. And of course I don't have a problem with it. I'd just like to be kept in the loop."

"Sorry," she said, fighting against the instinct to defend herself. "I was going to keep you in the loop. I didn't mean to keep you out of it. It was just in the early thought stages now."

"Okay. When you get further than the early stages, maybe you can let me know." He gave her a half smile that proved he wasn't unhappy with her.

She smiled back and let him pull her down to press

against him again. "I think this means you *will* miss me," she murmured.

"Maybe a little." He turned her over and pulled her up so he could kiss her, and the kiss was just getting deeper when they both froze at the sound of a girlish voice from the hallway.

"Daddy! Dad, where are you?"

Ellie didn't sound angry or whiney. She sounded scared.

"I'm here," Gabe called out loudly enough to be heard through the door. "I'm in here, Ellie." He rolled over and jumped to his feet, straightening his pants just as the door started to open.

He hurried over to where Ellie stood in the doorway, staring at them, her face a little pale. "I'm here, sweetheart. What's the matter?"

"Nothing." She rubbed at her nose. "I just didn't know where you were." Ellie looked over at Lydia, who had sat up in the bed, hoping she was mostly presentable. "Are you sleeping in late?"

"We were," she said with a smile, trying to sound natural. "But we had already woken up." She really hoped it wasn't going to upset Ellie to see that her father had slept in Lydia's room.

Ellie didn't seem to think it was strange that Gabe hadn't slept in his own bed. She was returning the hug he gave her, but she smiled over at Lydia. "I like your pajamas."

Lydia looked down at her pale blue, polar bear pajamas. "Thank you. You know, your dad has to go to a meeting for lunch, so I was thinking maybe you and I could do something fun. We could go visit Uncle Thomas and Mia if you want. He has a big huge yard that's really fun to explore."

Ellie nodded. "That would be fun. Thank you."

Lydia caught Gabe's eye, and they both smiled with their gazes alone. Ellie's attitude seemed to have changed for the better.

Maybe yesterday had been a turning point.

"Just be careful," Lydia called up to Ellie. "Don't put your weight on any branches that don't seem really strong."

"I won't." Ellie was climbing a big tree on Thomas's property. He owned a large, rambling house just outside of town, not far from their childhood home. Today was one of his days off, and he'd had Mia all week since Abigail was taking their daughter out of town starting tomorrow to visit her parents for Christmas.

Lydia and Ellie had arrived around eleven, and Ellie and Mia had played some—which mostly consisted of Ellie bossing the younger girl around.

Then Ellie had declared she'd wanted to explore the woods that were part of Thomas's property, so Lydia had taken her for a walk since Mia wanted to read instead.

"How high did you get?" Ellie called down. She was about halfway up the tree and climbing surprisingly well—since evidently she wasn't a well-practiced tree climber.

"I can't remember. Just go as high as you're comfortable." Lydia was regretting her random comment about loving to climb this particular tree when she was Ellie's age.

She'd climbed all the way to the top all the time though. And when no one else was around. The tree looked very tall, and Ellie looked very small, but surely it wasn't dangerous. Not if Lydia had done it so many times herself when she was even younger.

"I'm comfortable," Ellie called down.

Lydia reassured herself with the fact that the girl was doing fine. "Very good."

She stood under the tree watching Ellie, thinking back to when she was a girl. When she wanted to be alone, she would climb the tree and sit for over an hour sometimes, just thinking and watching the birds and bugs and leaves.

Ellie got about two-thirds of the way up the tree and stopped.

"Everything okay?" Lydia asked.

"Yes." Ellie was reaching up for another branch, but she kept pulling her arm back before she reached it. "I'm going to come down now."

"That's sounds like a good idea. You got up as high as I ever did." Lydia wasn't sure if this was entirely true, but she wanted to encourage the girl.

"Good."

Ellie was coming down now, just as fast as she'd climbed.

"There's no hurry," Lydia called, wincing slightly when Ellie almost missed a branch. "Take your time."

"I am taking my time."

Whether this was true or not, Lydia didn't argue. And she let out a sigh of relief when Ellie neared the bottom.

"That was fun," Ellie said with a smile, stretching her leg

down for the big branch Lydia had boosted her up to earlier. "I didn't know climbing trees was so much fun."

The girl definitely could have used a brother. Imagine never having climbed a tree at nine years old.

"I always liked it—Ellie, wait, not too fast!" Lydia jumped forward when Ellie's foot missed the branch below it and her small body slipped down too quickly from the branch above since she'd expected to be secured on the lower branch. Ellie's body jarred against the big branch from the fall and then kind of bounced off and down toward the ground.

Lydia was right beneath her, so Ellie landed on her hard. They both fell down to the ground.

"Ellie," Lydia gasped, trying to catch her breath and sit up. "Ellie, honey, are you okay?"

Ellie didn't answer. Her body was a dead weight on top of her.

Terrified, Lydia rearranged them so that Ellie was lying on the ground and she was sitting up so she could see.

There was blood streaming down over the girl's face. So much blood Lydia almost choked.

"Ellie," she rasped, trying to wipe the blood away from her closed eyes. "Ellie!"

There was no answer, and Lydia experienced a wave of pure terror at the thought that the girl might be dead. She wasn't though. She felt a pulse when she fumbled for Ellie's wrist, and she could see her chest rise and fall with her breath.

She must have knocked herself out on the big branch as she fell.

Still terrified, Lydia scrambled to her feet and reached

down to pick up Ellie. But then she stopped herself, hit with some vague memory that you weren't supposed to move people who had been injured for fear of making the injury worse.

Instead of reaching for Ellie, she reached for her phone and dialed her brother.

"What's going on?" Thomas said, picking up, clearly surprised by her call.

"Ellie fell out of a tree. The big oak tree in the southwest corner. She's bleeding terribly. She won't wake up!" The last sentence was a wail as Lydia's fear caught up with her.

"Don't move her," Thomas said, brisk and calm. "I'm on my way."

Lydia sat down next to Ellie, wiping the blood off her face as best she could and realizing the gash was just above her hairline.

She hadn't seen her head impact the tree, but it must have hit the branch or something on the way down.

Lydia prayed and trembled for three minutes until Thomas appeared. He must have run the whole way.

After a quick look at Lydia, he knelt down next to Ellie and started to examine her with professional calm.

"I think she's okay," he said after a minute.

Lydia choked back a sob of relief.

"She hit her head, so she must have a concussion, but she doesn't seem to have broken any bones. As long as she wakes up soon… Ellie." His voice was brisk and authoritative. "Ellie, wake up."

Ellie made a little sound in her throat.

Encouraged, Lydia moved closer. "Ellie, can you wake up, honey?"

"Wake up." Thomas's voice was much sterner than hers.

Ellie's eyes fluttered open, and Lydia almost dissolved in her immense relief.

"We should take her to the ER," Thomas said, looking over at Lydia. "Just to be safe."

"Yeah. Is it okay to move her?"

"Yeah. I think so. Ellie, does anything hurt?"

"My head." Ellie's face was twisted, and she looked pale and bewildered. "Did I fall down?"

"Yes, when you were climbing down the tree," Lydia said.

"You caught me?"

"Well, sort of. We both fell down." Lydia wished she could hug the little girl.

"You have a bump on your head," Thomas explained. "Does anything else hurt?"

"My wrist." She lifted her arm to show him.

He felt her wrist, and when she winced as he moved it a certain way, he said, "A little sprain, I think. Anything else?"

Lydia knew this side of her brother. Curt. Professional. Completely in control. It used to drive her crazy, but now it was exactly what she needed to get control of her fear.

"I don't think so."

"Can you move your legs?"

She shifted them around and nodded her head.

"And both arms?"

She moved them too.

"Very good. Can you turn your head from side to side?" When the girl did so, Thomas nodded. "Okay. You're in good shape, but I'm going to pick you up and carry you to the car if that's okay. I'm going to get a doctor to fix up your head."

"Aren't you a doctor?" Ellie's voice was weak, but she seemed to understand fine, which was a great relief.

"I'm a different kind of doctor. I'm only good if you need surgery on your heart. Do you need surgery on your heart?"

"No, thank you."

He chuckled and picked her up in his arms. Then he smiled over at Lydia. "Don't look so scared. She's going to be fine. We'll just stop to grab Mia, and we'll be on our way."

Lydia had no reason not to believe her brother, but she prayed all the way to the hospital anyway.

Three hours later, she was sitting next to Ellie's bed in the ER, so exhausted she wanted to drop.

Thomas had been right, and Ellie had a concussion. They didn't think it was serious, but they wanted to observe her for a while before they sent her home. She'd had to have six stitches to sew up the gash in her head.

Ellie had dozed off a few minutes ago, so Lydia had leaned her head back and closed her eyes. She'd called Gabe on the way to the hospital, and he'd gotten in his car to drive home immediately. He should be here soon.

She wished he was here now.

"Lydia," a soft, male voice came from the doorway.

She opened her eyes and straightened up with a jerk,

but it was just Thomas standing there. She stood up and walked over to him so their conversation wouldn't wake up Ellie. They stepped out into the hallway to talk.

"Are you okay?"

"Yeah. She's fine, I think. At least that's what everyone says."

'I know. She really is fine. I was asking how *you* are."

"Oh." She was kind of embarrassed since she felt uncharacteristically weak. "I'm fine."

"Do you need anything? Coffee or something?"

"No. I'm okay. I—" She broke off when a motion from down the hall distracted her.

Gabe. Striding down the hall toward them as if nothing could stand in his way.

She gave a little whimper at the sight of him, so glad was she to see him.

He pulled her into his arms as soon as he reached her, giving her a brief, hard hug.

"She's fine," Lydia said against his chest, unable to even imagine how she'd be having this conversation if Ellie hadn't been fine. "She's resting now, but she's fine."

She'd called to tell him, after she'd heard from the doctor, but she hadn't expected Gabe to relax until he could see his daughter for himself. He walked into the room and stared at Ellie, who was still sleeping.

"She's thinking well and seeing well and moving well," Thomas said from behind them. "No worries at all. Just the stitches and a headache."

Gabe took a raspy breath and nodded. Some of the tension in his body relaxed. Lydia could feel this palpably since his arm was still around her. "When did they say we can take her home?"

"In a few hours."

"Okay." Gabe went to sit down in the chair next to the bed and pulled Lydia down beside him even though there wasn't really room for both of them in the chair.

Thomas gave her a little smile. "I've got to get Mia home. Call me if you need me."

"Thanks, Thomas."

When he was gone, Gabe murmured, "What happened?"

Lydia gave him a fuller account than she'd been able to manage on the phone earlier, and Gabe just listened and nodded.

"I'm so sorry," Lydia concluded, her voice cracking. "I shouldn't have let her climb—"

"It wasn't your fault."

"It kind of was. I was the one who told her about climbing the tree. I was the one who let her. I didn't think it would be a problem, but I should have been smart—"

"Lydia, stop. She's fine. We can't protect her from everything." He leaned down to kiss her forehead softly. "All we can do is the best we can."

She exhaled, feeling better, but she couldn't help but wonder if he'd have come to the same conclusion if Ellie had been seriously hurt.

"I have to trust God with Ellie," he added, his voice rough with feeling. "There's no other way I could make it through the day."

Lydia nodded, understanding exactly what he was saying. And realizing that he was sharing with her one of the deepest truths of his life.

~

A little while later they went down to the cafeteria since Gabe insisted she needed something to eat.

Lydia didn't feel like eating, but she went anyway since she didn't have energy for an argument.

They picked out sandwiches and flavored waters and brought them over to the cash register. The woman who was supposed to be waiting on them was talking on a cell phone.

Lydia was briefly annoyed, but she didn't dwell on it. At least she didn't until they'd been waiting for a few minutes and the woman made no move to take their money.

She started to get tense as they continued to wait. She just wasn't up to controlling her impatience today. She was taking a breath to say something to get the woman to do her job when she felt Gabe's hand on her back.

She glanced up at him in surprise, but he wasn't even looking at her. He was checking something on his phone. Probably a text from Ellie's mother. He'd called her earlier to let her know what happened, and she always replied to his messages with just a text.

She didn't know why he'd put a hand on her back, but it reminded her that there was no reason to take out her bad day on some poor woman, so she bit back her pushy comment.

Fortunately, the woman hung up just then so Lydia could feel rewarded.

~

That night, Lydia went to bed absolutely exhausted.

They'd gotten Ellie home and watched TV with her for a while. But Lydia was so tired that she'd taken a shower and gone to bed just after Ellie had.

She felt weak and anxious and strangely confused, and she wanted Gabe desperately. But it had been just as hard a day for him as it had been for her, and she couldn't imagine he would be remotely interested in sex.

She wasn't in the mood either. She just wanted to be with him.

But she huddled under her covers, still praying and hoping she'd be able to sleep.

She was still awake an hour later when there was a soft knock on the door.

"Yes?" She sat up in her bed, surprised and confused.

The door swung open, and Gabe stood silhouetted by the light from the hallway.

"You can come in," she said when he just stood there.

"Did I wake you up?" He took a few steps into her dark room.

"No. I wasn't sleeping. Did you want to—" She stretched an arm out toward him.

He closed the door behind him and made his way to her bed. Then he climbed under the covers and pulled her into his arms.

She exhaled loudly and snuggled against him.

"I thought you might come to my room tonight," he murmured, tightening his arms around her almost painfully.

"I didn't think you'd feel like sex."

"I don't. I don't."

And she realized then that he hadn't come to her for sex. He'd come to her for comfort. The same comfort she needed herself. She made a little whimper.

"Are you okay?" he murmured.

"Yeah. I was so scared. I was... so scared."

"I know. So was I." He adjusted her so he could hold her more comfortably, his body relaxing a little. "Do you ever cry?"

"No. Not really. Not much. Occasionally, but not much. But I felt like it today."

"Me too," he admitted. "For so long, she's been all I've had."

"I know."

He leaned down to kiss her. "And it's so strange that now I have you too."

"You do have me," she murmured, clinging to his big, warm body. "I hope you know that."

He didn't answer, just held her even tighter, like he couldn't seem to let her go. The urgency in his grip thrilled and terrified her both. She wanted his need—it matched her own—but she couldn't help but wonder if he was afraid she would slip out of his grip.

She wanted him to trust her.

She wanted him to know she wasn't going to leave.

She wanted him to trust God with their marriage, the same way he trusted God with the other parts of his life.

And she just wasn't sure if he did.

CHAPTER 11

T̲HE NEXT MORNING WAS C̲HRISTMAS E̲VE.

Lydia woke up to find that Gabe wasn't in bed with her, and she was ludicrously disappointed. She hoped he hadn't gone back to his own bed to sleep sometime during the night, although it was certainly possible, and she had no grounds to complain even if he had.

Theirs was a marriage of convenience, after all. A practical marriage with no emotional expectations. Either of them could sleep on their own if they wanted.

Lydia just didn't really want to anymore.

She sighed and stretched, suddenly remembering that poor little Ellie had fallen out of a tree the day before. Lydia jumped up and sprinted up to the third floor to check on her.

In the doorway, she collided with Gabe, who was just leaving the room.

"Oomph," she gasped as Gabe reached to stabilize her after the impact.

"You okay?" Gabe was wearing his pajamas. He'd obviously done the same thing she had on waking up.

"Yeah." She kept her voice low so as not to wake Ellie, who was sleeping on her bed across the room. "Just coming to check on her. Is she okay?"

"She's fine. Let's let her sleep longer." He put his hand on her back as they walked back down the stairs, and then he came into the bedroom with her on the second floor.

Since it wasn't even six yet, Lydia crawled back under the covers, and she smiled when Gabe got back in bed with her.

She scooted over to nestle against him.

Gabe wrapped his arm around her, and they lay together in pleasant silence for several minutes.

Then, following the line of her thoughts, Lydia asked, "Do you think Ellie will be up to singing in the Christmas Eve service tonight?"

"I hope so. We'll just let her decide."

"She's been really excited about it."

"I know. Hopefully, she'll feel up to it."

"She's a good little girl." Lydia smiled at the thought of Ellie. She'd met the girl for the first time less than three months ago, and she already cared about her a lot. So much so that she was actually dreading the idea of being away from her so long during the year when she was in India and Ellie was going to school here.

She was also dreading being away from Gabe.

"I know she is," Gabe said. "Thanks for being so good with her."

"I don't think I'm that good." Lydia shifted to look up at his face. "I've got a lot of learning yet to do."

He shook his head, his expression fond. "You've been great. And I'm so grateful that she'll have a woman in her life who she can look up to—especially as she starts to get older." He sighed. "Sometimes it terrifies me to think of what I'll do when she's a teenager."

"You're wonderful with her. You're a wonderful father." She reached up to stroke his bristly cheek. "I'm really happy to be part of her life, but you'd be fine even without me."

There was something in his expression now that made her heart feel like it was flying. "Maybe. But I'm even better with you."

She took a shaky breath, almost dizzy from the emotions. "Me too."

He smiled and looked like he did when he kissed her, but he didn't pull her up to his mouth. Just kept gazing at her.

"I kind of love her, you know," Lydia said, so full of feeling she had to express it. She'd always been honest and forthright, and there didn't seem to be a good reason not to be now.

His smiled broadened. "I know. You have no idea how much that means to me."

She cleared her throat. "Well, you know..." She trailed off, hesitating for the first time since what she was going to say felt so big. But it was true. It was *true*.

So she said it.

"And I kind of love you too."

She saw a fire blaze up in his eyes for just a moment at her words. She was sure she didn't imagine it. But then she saw a clear sequence of emotions follow the initial reaction.

His face was just as hard to read as it had ever been, but she knew him now. And so she saw and understood each emotion as it passed to the next.

Recognition. Surprise. Confusion. Fear. Withdrawal. Fear. Fear. *Fear.*

And the flying of her heart suddenly dropped with a sickening thud.

"What?" he asked, the word strangling a little in his throat.

She gave a little cough, suddenly wishing she hadn't said it. Things had been so good, and she'd just ruined it.

Sometimes being open about everything that went through her mind wasn't the best thing to do. She'd learned that as she'd grown up.

She should have learned it better.

"Nothing." She glanced away, something aching in her throat that was difficult to speak over. "I was just... It's no big deal."

"But you said—"

"Don't worry about what I said. It was just a passing thought." She tried to smile at him naturally although she felt crushed. Devastated. She pulled away from him and sat up on the bed, hoping the position would get her mind to work better.

Gabe sat up too, looking at her soberly. The fear she'd seen in his eyes had disappeared, but so had all the feeling she'd seen before. "You're not expecting..."

"I'm not expecting anything. Things are great between

us." Her cheekbones ached from trying to keep her face in a smile.

"Because this marriage was always—"

"Practical," she interrupted. "I know. I'm not complaining or expecting anything else. I'm *not*."

"Okay." He took a strange, shuddering breath. "Because I told you from the beginning that I don't think I can trust another woman with—"

"Your heart." She knew she was finishing his sentences, but she just needed to get this conversation over with. "I know. I'm not expecting you to trust me with your heart. I'm not expecting *anything*. I'm sorry I said anything. Things are great between us."

She knew exactly what had happened. He'd suddenly realized that they were getting too close, and his heart was potentially in danger. And he'd retreated.

After what had happened with his first wife, she could hardly blame him.

And if it cracked her heart to think that he didn't believe he could trust her with what was most important, then that was her own fault.

She'd known what she was doing when she entered this marriage.

"Are you sure?" Gabe looked stiff, awkward, horribly uncomfortable. "Because I thought we understood each other. But if you—"

"I do understand. Stop obsessing about one random comment. How many times do I have to say that everything is fine?" She got out of bed, needing to escape from this conversation. Really soon.

"Okay," he said slowly, getting up too. "Maybe we

should take a step back, just to make sure things are okay between us. I don't want there to be any confusion."

And that hurt even more although she should have known he would do that. Because he'd suddenly realized what was happening between them, and it terrified him.

"Okay." She nodded and headed for her bathroom. "That's a good idea. I'm going to take a shower now."

Her departure was kind of rude and abrupt, but she didn't have a choice. She had to get away from him before she started to cry.

She'd just been telling him yesterday that she never cried.

She was fully dressed in jeans and a sweatshirt when she came downstairs an hour later.

Gabe and Ellie were at the kitchen table, with the remains of waffles on their plates and a tablet between them. They were obviously playing a game together.

They looked so domestic, so dear, that she felt a hard pain in her throat at the sight. They looked like a family—a family she had never really been a part of. But she pushed through her reaction.

She might have cried—just a little—in the shower, but she wasn't a fool or a child. If Gabe didn't want their marriage to get any closer, then she could live with that.

After all, in a few months she'd be heading to India and she could start over there. She could focus on her work—the most important thing—and the family she didn't have after all simply wouldn't matter that much.

She'd lived for several years convinced she would never have the kind of marriage so many other women had. She'd thought that meant she would never be married at all. Now she realized she hadn't been wrong. Even though she was married, her initial understanding had been correct.

Her life wouldn't be about loving a husband and family. It would be about her work. She'd always been satisfied with that.

She could be satisfied with it now.

All of this processed in her mind as she stood briefly and watched them.

Then Gabe looked up and saw her, and she smiled brightly. "Good morning! How are you feeling, Ellie?"

The girl looked up with a smile. She had a big bandage on her forehead, and her hair was a tangled mess. But she looked a lot better than she had the day before. "I'm doing fine. My head doesn't hurt today, but it feels weird around my stitches. Daddy says that's normal."

"I think it is. I'm glad you're feeling better." She could feel Gabe watching her, but she kept her eyes on Ellie. "I hope you'll feel up to singing at church tonight."

"I will. I'm sure I'll feel up to it tonight."

"Good."

"Aren't you going to make her a waffle?" Ellie asked, turning to her father.

"Sure," Gabe said, starting to get up. On the surface, he looked natural, but she could tell that he'd withdrawn. Like he was hiding himself behind his quiet reserve, the way he had at the beginning.

Lydia hated the sight of it, but she reminded herself it

was no big deal. "I don't need a waffle," she said quickly. "I'm not very hungry this morning." She went to get herself some coffee, hoping it would clear the painful fog in her head.

"Oh. But they were really good," Ellie said. "Dad makes the best waffles."

"I'm sure they were. But I'm not very hungry."

She got her coffee and then made herself a piece of toast, but even the normal activities felt fake somehow, as if it wasn't real, as if none of this was real, as if she was just going through the motions, as if this wasn't really *her* at all.

She tried to look at Gabe a couple of times to prove that everything was fine, but it was too painful, so she mostly just avoided his eyes.

She sat down at the table, and they had a conversation about their plans for the day. And all the time the pain in her chest and the lump in her gut only intensified.

It felt like Gabe wasn't really with her, even though he was sitting about a foot away from her. It felt like she wasn't really with either of them—as if she were an outsider intruding on their family.

It shouldn't matter to her, but it did.

"What's wrong?" Ellie asked after a stretch of tense silence.

"Nothing is wrong," Gabe told her.

"Something feels wrong." Ellie looked between the two of them. "Are you fighting?"

Lydia gave her another bright smile. "We're not fighting. We were having a normal conversation, weren't we?"

The girl's brow lowered dubiously. "Something seems wrong."

And that hurt too since the idea obviously worried her. Lydia wanted to comfort and reassure her, but there was nothing she could do. Nothing she could say.

Something *was* wrong. At least it was wronger than it had been the day before. But it wasn't something Lydia could fix.

It had been Gabe's decision, and now they all had to live it out.

Lydia wrapped presents in the morning, mostly so she could be alone. She'd bought some for her own family—her real family—and also a few for Gabe and Ellie. Then she went to have lunch with her parents, as another excuse to get away.

She was convinced she would eventually be perfectly happy with this situation—it would just take a little transition time.

Obviously, her emotions were far more involved here than she'd ever intended.

But she'd never been a particularly emotional woman. She could deal with this, just like she'd dealt with everything she'd faced before.

When she returned to the house, Ellie wanted her to play a board game with her and Gabe, and Lydia forced herself not to refuse. She didn't want to ruin the girl's Christmas, after all.

Lydia managed to focus on the game and on Ellie, and not to focus on Gabe very much, so she got through the game without revealing anything she was feeling.

She went to the kitchen to get Ellie some cookies and hot chocolate afterward, feeling pretty proud of herself that she'd managed to get through the day without breaking down or making a fool of herself.

After a couple of days, she would feel better. Then her life could go back to the way it had always been before.

She was going to India. Her life had been set on that goal for so long. Nothing that had happened in the past couple of months was going to change it.

"Lydia."

She almost jumped at the shock of hearing the low voice behind her. She obviously knew who it was. She took a deep breath and kept counting out a few cookies from the pack.

"Lydia," Gabe murmured again, coming over to stand very close to her.

Way too close.

Lydia turned to face him without really looking at him. "Yes?" Ellie was in the other room, but she didn't want there to be a chance that they were overheard.

"Are you okay?" Gabe asked, his blue eyes searching her face.

Lydia suddenly wanted to scream—in absolute frustration. How the hell did he expect her to be okay after what had happened this morning. She took another deep breath, however, and managed to say calmly, "I'm fine. I told you that before."

He leaned in closer. "I'm sorry about everything. I don't know… I mean, I didn't want to mess things up between us."

With great restraint, she managed not to say that he'd

succeeded in doing so anyway. She had no right to complain. Their marriage was exactly what they'd agreed on, and she could hardly reproach him for that. "It's fine. How many times do I have to tell you?"

"But it feels like it's *not* fine." He was big and warm and tense and right there. His heavy-lidded eyes seemed to see far too much, all the way into her heart, her soul. She couldn't seem to get away from him.

"I'm sorry." Her voice broke, but she pushed through the ache in her throat. "But I don't know what you expect of me. You can't have it both ways. I can't be close to you if you won't let me be close to you. I'm okay with whatever you decide, but you can't expect it to be like it was before, when you're the one who put the barrier between us."

He stared at her, his eyes strangely agonized. "It's not that easy," he said at last, his voice very thick.

"I know it's not. I know it's not easy. And you're right, the easiest thing is for us to not be close. It will be easier for us to just live our own lives—on our own except for what we originally agreed—so that's what we'll do."

Lydia pushed him back gently so she could get away, and then she carried the cookies and mug back to the living room where Ellie was waiting.

And it was fine. It was all fine.

If she repeated it often enough, maybe she could convince Gabe.

Maybe she could convince herself too.

❧

By the time she and Gabe were sitting side by side at the Christmas Eve service that evening, Lydia was about ready to crack.

She couldn't remember a harder day in her life—like every little thing she did was stretching her beyond the boundaries of her being.

Gabe felt like a stranger beside her, and all of it felt wrong to the core—like this wasn't really who they were, like it wasn't who they were supposed to be. But she kept telling herself it was what it was, and there was no use in trying to change it.

Ellie did a good job with her singing, and then she came back to sit on the other side of Gabe in the pew. The rest of the service was readings and carols, and they ended with the traditional candle-lighting as the congregation sang "Silent Night."

Lydia had always loved the Christmas Eve service at this church, and she tried desperately to focus on worship. Christmas wasn't about her sham of a marriage, and it wasn't about what felt like a broken heart.

It was about Jesus coming into the world to save it, to save her. She wrenched her mind away from Gabe and Ellie so she could focus on the service.

But, by the end, emotion was bleak and heavy in her throat, her chest, her eyes, and she couldn't even finish the final verse of "Silent Night."

Gabe hadn't even tried to sing. She hadn't looked at him once, but she was conscious of every move he made. He stood beside her like a statue, staring down at the hymnal he was holding low so Ellie could see the words too.

After Daniel gave the benediction, Gabe reached out to

pull her against him and tilted his head to say in her ear, "Lydia."

It was obviously the beginning of a question, so she didn't let him finish it. Her body tensed up, keeping herself from touching him more than she had to. She couldn't be so close to him. She was already too far stretched, and she couldn't take anything more. "I said I'm fine," she whispered. "Don't you dare ask me again."

"I wasn't—"

"Go ahead and take Ellie home," she said, trying not to look at him even as she was speaking into his ear. "I'll get Thomas to take me back. He's on his own, so I don't want him to feel lonely." It was true, but it was a flimsy excuse. Gabe would obviously know the pretext for what it was.

"Lydia." Gabe's body was so tense he was almost shaking with it.

"I'm sorry. You can't have it both ways, and you need to give me a little time. I'm sorry." She pulled away from him and leaned down to give Ellie a hug, telling the girl she'd done a wonderful job with her singing and she'd see her at home.

Ellie looked a little worried, but Lydia couldn't help that.

She couldn't seem to help anything. She just wanted this damned day to be over at last.

She went to the restroom to kill some time, and she was relieved when Gabe and Ellie were gone by the time she came out.

Then she talked some with her parents, trying desperately to act cheerful, and she finally went to find Thomas, who was sitting on the stoop outside the back door of the church.

It was chilly and clear outside, the moon and stars very bright. Lydia sat down next to him even though the concrete was cold and uncomfortable.

He gave her a wry smile. "So what's going on?"

"What do you mean?"

"I'm sure it's possible you feel sorry for me since I can't spend Christmas with my wife and daughter—"

"I don't feel sor—"

"But that's not why you didn't go home with your own family tonight." His green eyes had always been deep and clever, but right now they seemed unnaturally experienced, almost weary from it.

Lydia let out a sigh, fighting that same ache in her chest and lump in her gut. "They're not really my family. *You're* my family."

He gave her a sharp look. "They're your family now. What's wrong?"

"Nothing. I mean, nothing important." The breeze against her face was brisk and biting, but she was chilled for a different reason, like a fire somewhere inside her had gone out.

"Gabe and Ellie are very important."

"I know. I didn't mean that. It's just that…"

"Just that what?"

She blew out a long sigh. "Things never work out the way they're supposed to, do they?"

"No. They never do." He studied her face. "What happened?"

She wasn't sure how to answer the question, but she tried—as always—to be honest. "It's a complicated situation. My marriage, I mean. And I'm trying to do the right thing. But I guess the right thing doesn't *feel* like the right thing."

"I don't know what that means."

"I know. I don't know how to explain it. I just want to do the right thing."

"Well, that's easy." Thomas turned his head to stare down at the pavement of the parking lot. "You love them. *That's* the right thing."

For some reason the words hurt so much she almost shook with it. "It's not that easy."

"I didn't say it was easy. Anyone who says that loving someone else is easy has never really done it. It's not easy. It's *right*." He turned back to look at her, suddenly urgent. "Believe me. What's easy is being selfish. What's easy is trashing your marriage. That's the easiest thing to do, and then you've made mistakes that just can't be taken back."

Thomas had never talked to her—to anyone—about what had happened with his marriage, and Lydia was suddenly distracted from her own grief and confusion by a wave of intense sympathy. "Thomas, you didn't—"

"I didn't cheat on her. I never cheated. I never even wanted to. But there are plenty of other ways to trash your marriage. And then it's like moving a mountain, trying to fix things. Trying to mend the hurt you've caused. And some things just can't be fixed. Can't be mended."

"I'm so sorry," she murmured, her voice cracking. "You still love her?"

"Of course I still love her. But she doesn't trust me, and I can hardly blame her for that."

"Shit." She reached out to squeeze his arm.

"Yeah. But the point is not to feel sorry for me. The point is to not do the same thing. Whatever happened, go back home and try to fix it while it can still be fixed."

"That sounds like good advice." The voice surprised both of them, coming from behind them. They turned to see Daniel, who had evidently come out the back door.

"Sorry," Daniel said, stepping down to the pavement and lowering himself to sit beside them on the stoop. "I didn't mean to eavesdrop. I only heard the end of it anyway."

"It's fine." She smiled at Daniel, who was a good man and a wise man and a friend. "I'm just having some marriage problems, and Thomas was trying to help."

"Despite the appalling irony of my helping anyone with their marriage," Thomas added.

Daniel gave them a faint smile. "For what it's worth, I did a pretty good job trying to trash my marriage too, and it's only grace that I didn't succeed."

Lydia chuckled. "Thanks for saying that, but I don't believe you for a moment."

Daniel and Jessica had the kind of marriage she'd never imagined she could have. Only lately—only just recently—had she started to want that kind of marriage, but she'd been right all along about it never being intended for her.

She slumped, suddenly overwhelmed by how terrible it felt. That she could never have that kind of marriage with Gabe.

"It's fine," she said as if someone else had spoken. "It's okay. It doesn't really matter. I'll do the best I can, but I'll be heading to India this summer. That's what's important to me."

She was speaking mostly to herself, and she probably wouldn't have said it out loud if she'd thought about it, if she'd had her normal emotional barriers intact.

But there was a strange tense silence that followed, as if the men had heard her, were silently responding to the words.

Before anyone could say anything, Jessica came out the door, smiling and very pregnant, and Daniel stood up.

"There you are," Jessica said, taking Daniel's arm. "I was about to leave and make you run all the way home again."

Lydia was faintly interested in the "again"—wondering when Jessica had made Daniel run home in the first place —but there was too much else going on in her mind for her to worry about it.

Daniel tilted his head to kiss his wife, but then he turned back to look down at Lydia. "You know, God didn't save the world with a magic wand."

She blinked at him. "What?"

"He didn't save the world with a magic wand," Daniel repeated, his voice taking on a powerful sort of gravity, even though it was still soft. "He could have, but he didn't. He was born a baby. Think about what that means. What do you think we were doing in there tonight?" He nodded toward the church building.

Lydia shook her head, feeling helpless, so sad. "I don't know what you mean."

"He took on flesh. He took *our* flesh. He lived our life. He breathed our breath." Daniel's brown eyes held hers without wavering. "He ate bread, and he drank wine, and he built things with iron and wood."

She stared at him, feeling breathless, like something really important was about to happen.

"And he laughed when it was a funny, and he cried when it hurt. And he kissed and hugged the people he loved. He bled when he died." Daniel paused to take a breath. "He took on flesh, Lydia. He *lived* for thirty years before he started to preach. Think about what that means. And then tell me that living your life—right now, every day —doesn't really matter. That loving your husband and that girl who is now your daughter isn't really that important."

Lydia literally couldn't breathe. The world suddenly spun around her. She had been right and so incredibly wrong. Everything *had* changed.

"He didn't save the world with a magic wand," Daniel said one more time.

The silence stretched out for a long time.

Then Jessica said, "I have no idea what this is about, but sometimes he gets it right." She smiled up at her husband with obvious affection. "Sometimes he's worth listening to." She then gave Lydia a slightly teary smile.

Lydia stared at her, and then she turned to look at her brother.

He gave her a little nod.

"Okay. Okay. I get it." Her voice didn't even sound like herself. She stood up. "I better get home."

Thomas stood up too. "I'll take you there."

CHAPTER 12

FIVE MINUTES LATER, LYDIA WAS WALKING THROUGH THE door of their home.

She used to think about it as Gabe's house, but it was her house too. It felt like hers now. Like *theirs*.

It was completely silent, and she realized that Gabe must have convinced Ellie to go to bed early. The first floor of the house was dark except for the entryway light.

So Lydia put down her purse and went upstairs, discovering that Gabe's bedroom door was closed. A light was visible through the crack at the floor, the way she'd seen it so often.

She stood for a moment, suddenly terrified.

She wasn't the sort of person who normally hesitated before doing what she believed needed to be done. She wasn't the sort of person who was constantly fighting tears whenever she felt strong emotion. She wasn't the sort of person who was accustomed to feeling helpless.

But she did. Now. All of them. As she paused in front of Gabe's door.

This morning it felt like her heart had been broken, and she didn't want it to happen again.

But she made herself knock on the door anyway.

She heard a noise from inside. It wasn't even nine o'clock yet, so she was sure Gabe wouldn't be asleep yet. She wondered if he was hurting like she was.

It was a minute before the door swung open and Gabe stood before her.

He was still dressed, and he looked rumpled and exhausted and confused and stretched and like he really needed to shave. He looked like Gabe.

Like *Gabe*.

He just stared at her.

Finally, she made her voice work. "Sorry. Were you in bed or… or something?"

He shook his head and opened his mouth, but no words came out. His eyelids were heavier than she'd ever seen them before.

"I just wanted to say…" She stopped to clear her throat, mostly as a filler. "I know what you said this morning, and I can accept it. But it doesn't change how I feel about you and Ellie. I know you said we should take a step back, and you can do that if you need to, but I'm not going to do it."

He kept staring at her, frozen, speechless.

It was very unnerving, but she pressed on. "I think you're wrong about holding back—about not loving the people you've been given. And for whatever reason we got married, we were still given each other. But I can understand you've been hurt, and it's hard for you to trust me. I hope that will change. I think maybe it will. But I can wait. I can be patient. I'm not going to pull away."

She paused, hoping he'd say something, but he didn't move even an eyelash.

She took a shaky breath. "Anyway, that's all I wanted to say. You can work out whatever you need to work out for yourself. But I'm your wife. And I love you. And I'm not going anywhere."

To her absolute astonishment, her voice broke on the last two words and a tear slipped out of her eye to slide down her cheek.

Gabe stared at her, stared at the tear, and slowly lifted a hand to thumb it away. Then something seemed to crack in his composure without warning.

He made a rough, guttural sound and pulled her into his arms, holding her so tightly she couldn't breathe.

"Oh, baby, I love you too," he murmured, burying his face in her hair.

She was shaking—almost sobbing—and it was absolutely ridiculous. She wasn't this sort of person at all. She couldn't seem to stop though. When she pulled away at last, she was sniffing and beaming at the same time. "Do you mean it?"

"Yeah. I do. I'm absolutely crazy about you." He cupped her face with both of his hands. "I'm so sorry I pulled away. I was scared."

"I know. I understood."

"But it didn't make it right. Not when you're everything I never dared to even ask for."

Shivers of joy were running through her, and she wiped away a couple of stray tears. "Me too. Me either. Or whatever it should be. I had no idea I even wanted you, and now

I'm not sure how I lived without you. Are you sure you're not just overcome by my decline into tears?"

He chuckled and pulled her into another hug. "That did kind of drive the point home, but I was already going to tell you."

"Sure you were." She was feeling better—more herself— so she pulled back and gave him a teasing look as she closed the bedroom door behind her. "You're just trying to take my accolades for being the first one to make the move."

"I really was going to." He glanced back to the corner of the room where there was a small desk by the window. "I have written evidence, so you can never doubt me."

"Really?" She peered over and saw a piece of paper on the desk. "What evidence?"

"I was writing you a letter," he admitted a little sheepishly.

She gasped in shock and started over to look at the paper.

He grabbed her to hold her back. "No need to read it now."

"What do you mean? I want to read it."

"But I told you in person, so there's no reason to read the words." He still looked slightly awkward and self-conscious. "I was upset. Really upset. It might be kind of embarrassing."

She giggled and pulled out of his arms, running over to the desk before he caught her again. They had a little scuffle over the letter, but he eventually gave up and let her read.

It was only partly finished, but she scanned the lines and felt a swell of emotion rising in her throat.

"Don't make a big deal about it or anything," he muttered, reaching for it again although not persisting when she stretched her arm out to evade his grasp.

"Why would I make a big deal about it?" She read over the lines again. "It's not like you wrote me poetry or anything."

The words weren't poetry. They were blunt and to the point and full of obvious emotion.

I'm sorry. I love you. You must know how much I love you. I was just afraid of how much I was feeling for you and terrified that I would lose you. I didn't trust you, and I didn't trust God, and it was wrong. But I want to take the risk. I want to love you all the way. If you can forgive me for being an ass, I will show you how much I...

The letter stopped there. Lydia's eyes blurred slightly as she read it again.

"I told you not to make a big deal." He looked highly uncomfortable. "I wasn't supposed to be in the same room when you read it."

"Why were you writing a letter in the first place?"

"Because I was afraid I'd never get the words said otherwise. This way, it would be done, and I couldn't chicken out."

She smiled rather besottedly down at the wrinkled page. "It's like a Jane Austen novel."

Gabe groaned dramatically. "Please don't say that. It's just a stupid note. Here, give it back to me and I'll thro—"

"No!" She held the letter to her chest. "You're not going to throw it away. I'm going to keep it forever."

He rolled his eyes. "Okay, fine. You can keep it. But can you please at least put it down now?"

"Why?"

"Because I want to kiss you, and it's getting in the way."

She set down the letter on the desk, laughing uninhibitedly and then squealing when he grabbed her and pulled her down onto the bed with him.

He settled on top of her, gazing at her with his heart in his eyes. "I do love you. I hope you believe me."

"I do." She wrapped her arms around his neck. "I kind of knew it already although I didn't think you were ready to accept it yet. But now I have written evidence of that fact that I can save for posterity."

She giggled when he tried to glare at her.

"But seriously," he went on after a minute. "I want to be your husband for real. I won't hold anything back. And I know it means you could break my heart if you want t—"

"I'm never going to—"

"I know it's a risk, and I shouldn't have been scared to take it. You've made everything about my life better."

"Me too." Her face twisted briefly.

"Don't start crying again, or I'll get totally freaked out."

She made a choked sound and tangled her fingers in his thick hair. "I'm not crying. I'm so happy I could almost burst."

"That's okay then." He leaned down to kiss her. "And I know you have a heart to work in India, and that means we'll have to be apart some during the school year. And that's fine. We'll work it out. I want you to have everything. I want you to be able to do everything—I just want that everything to also include being my wife."

"Of course it means being your wife. What do you think I meant back there? I do want to work in India, and I think I can do some good there. I'm not going to give that up. But it doesn't have to look exactly the way I thought it would. Maybe I could work it out so I'm only there half the year. I'll talk to them. I don't want to be away from you and Ellie for that long. I want to have India and you and Ellie too if I can."

"Then you will," he said hoarsely, leaning to kiss her again. "We'll do whatever we need to, to make it work."

She pulled his head down because she wanted to kiss him again. And then the kiss deepened until neither could keep talking anymore.

Soon they were pulling off each other's clothes and kissing and caressing with almost frantic need.

When Gabe slid himself inside her, Lydia arched up and gasped out his name.

"Lydia," Gabe mumbled against her skin, his face buried in her neck as he held himself so tensely he was shaking with it. "I love you. I love you."

She arched again in pleasure at the sound of his saying the words.

He was filling her completely—tight and aching and unbearably good. And she was flushed with heat and urgency and already clawing at his shoulders.

When he began to thrust at last, they built up a fast, hungry rhythm—Gabe grunting out primitive sounds of effort and pleasure and Lydia biting her lower lip to keep from crying out.

She couldn't restrain the impulse for long, but it didn't seem to matter. Gabe was just as out of control as she was as they moved eagerly together, their damp skin clinging and their bodies slapping on each instroke.

Every time he pushed into her, Gabe rasped out, "I love you," and every time she heard it, Lydia cried out, "Yes!"

She was on the verge of coming when she met and held his gaze. His blue eyes were hot and needy, and they didn't look away from hers.

He was seeing her for real—in all her brokenness and humanness and messy feelings. He was making love to who she really was. Lydia came on the knowledge.

Gabe followed quickly, her clenching, shuddering body pulling him into climax as well.

She clung to him as she came down, her chest aching with breathlessness and her body so hot she thought she might melt. But she loved the feel of him, his heated, sated weight on top of her, the way he seemed to have let himself go completely.

Like he understood that she was making love to *him*—in all of his brokenness, humanness, and messiness—too.

Gabe buried his face in the crook of her neck again and mumbled against her throat, "Lydia, Lydia."

She arched her neck into his fumbling kisses. "Oh, Gabe, I love you so much."

He murmured his agreement, still pressing his lips against her flushed skin. Then he raised his head and said, a familiar dryness to his voice, "This might be the best Christmas ever."

Lydia could hardly disagree.

$\sim$

The next morning, she woke up to find that Gabe was already awake, lying in bed and watching her.

She smiled, remembering everything that had happened, how what was broken between them had been miraculously remade.

He smiled back. "Good morning."

"Good morning to you." She scooted over a little closer to him.

"Merry Christmas."

"Merry Christmas to you." She was having trouble containing her happiness. While it was unlikely she would feel this level of joy for a long time, she was definitely going to enjoy it for the time being.

"You look happy."

"I am happy." She recognized an answering feeling in his own eyes, so she added, "You look happy too."

"I'm glad we're on the same page."

She couldn't help but laugh. "I got you a really good present."

"I would certainly hope so." He did a pretty good job of looking aloof until he added, "What did you get me?"

"I'm not going to just come out and tell you."

"Why not?"

"Because it's a present. It's under the tree. You have to wait to open it. And don't forget to act surprised when you open Ellie's tie for you."

"I know. I'm good at acting surprised."

"I supposed you just acted surprised last night when I showed up at your door to make me feel better."

"Right. That's exactly what happened." His lips and eyes were both smiling.

"Liar."

"Okay, fine. I was so shocked and overjoyed I couldn't even move. But I'm well known for my composure and aplomb in the corporate world, so let's try not to let the news get around."

She giggled and rolled over on top of him. "You're well known for your aplomb, are you?"

"Right." His hands settled on her hips.

"Maybe I should discover how much aplomb you really have."

His eyes got suddenly hot. "Go right ahead."

"Dad? Aunt Lydia?" The voice was just outside the door.

Gabe smothered a groan, and Lydia giggled as she rolled off him.

"Come on in, Ellie," Gabe called out, sitting up in the bed.

Ellie opened the door. "Oh good," she said, grinning at them. "You're in bed. Stay there and don't move."

Lydia and Gabe gave each other questioning looks, but they did as she'd instructed as Ellie disappeared.

They heard her running down the stairs. After a minute, they heard her coming back up more slowly.

She appeared carrying, very carefully, a loaded tray in her arms. "I made you breakfast in bed for Christmas!"

Lydia gasped in surprise and turned to look at Gabe, who was obviously just as surprised as she was.

"Thank you so much," Gabe said as the girl walked over to the bed. "You didn't have to do that."

"I wanted to. It seemed like a Christmas-y thing to do." Ellie was beaming at them.

"No one has ever made me breakfast in bed before," Lydia said. "I'm so excited about it!"

Lydia's smile faltered in astonishment and feeling when she saw the frozen waffles that Ellie had toasted and plated up on the tray.

They were decorated with berries, whipped cream from a spray container, and chocolate syrup.

She'd written "Dad" on Gabe's waffle and "Mom" on what must be Lydia's.

"I know you're not my mom for real," Ellie said seriously, looking nervously from the waffle to Lydia's face. "But I couldn't fit Aunt Lydia on it, but you act like a mom to me now, so I thought it might be okay." She took a strange, shaky breath. "Is that okay?"

Lydia raised a hand to cover her mouth, frozen by the crashing wave of emotion.

"Is that okay?" Ellie asked again, looking nervously from her father to Lydia.

"Of course it's okay," Gabe said rather hoarsely. He pulled Ellie onto the bed and gave her a one-armed hug. "Of course it's okay. She's just really touched by it. Aren't you?"

Lydia nodded, lowering her hand and pulling herself together. "I am. Thank you so much, honey. I love that you put that on my waffle. And you can call me that if you want. Or anything you want."

Ellie's pretty face relaxed, and she scooted over her father to hug Lydia, almost toppling the tray in the process. "Good," the girl said, settling herself between them. "I'm glad you married Dad, and I'm glad you're having Christmas with us."

"I'm glad too." Lydia was so full of feeling she'd lost her typical practical, no-nonsense attitude, but she assumed it would come back eventually.

"And I'm glad too," Gabe put in, "so we're all agreed. Did you want to say a prayer for the food?"

Ellie agreed and bowed her head to thank God for the waffles and the whipped cream and for Christmas and for Lydia and for her daddy and for the baby Jesus.

Gabe met Lydia's eyes over his daughter's head as Ellie said, "Amen," and Lydia could see clearly see how full of joy and awe he was this morning.

It made sense to her since she felt exactly the same way.

So they had the waffles, which were admittedly overly sweet and no longer warm. But Lydia had never enjoyed a breakfast—on Christmas morning or any other morning—more than she did that one.

They were finished, and Ellie had carried the tray downstairs to the kitchen and was back to try to hurry them up so they could go downstairs to open presents, when the doorbell rang.

They all looked at each other in surprise for a moment. Then Lydia decided she was more presentable at the moment than Gabe, so she got up to go see who it was.

Thomas was on the front doorstep with a pan of their mother's cinnamon rolls.

"They're still warm," he said with a grin. "Mom said I had to take them over right away and insisted you wouldn't be still asleep."

Lydia laughed and gave him a hug, which he returned with one arm. "We weren't asleep. Merry Christmas. Come on in."

He walked into the kitchen with her and set the pan on the counter. Glancing around at the quiet house, he asked softly, "So is everything all right?"

"Yes," she said, unable to keep from smiling like an idiot. "It's all good."

His eyes rested on her face for a moment, and then he smiled too. "Good for you. I'm really glad."

She understood that he was glad, but there was also an underlying poignancy to his expression that made her heart go out to him. She couldn't imagine how hard it would be to not be allowed to spend Christmas with Gabe and Ellie.

"We were about to open presents," she said, reaching out to squeeze his arm. "Why don't you stay and join us."

He shook his head. "It's your first Christmas. You should do it as a family." When she started to object, he went on, "I'm fine, Lydia. Seriously. Mom and Dad are expecting me back at their place, and I've got to call Mia in a few minutes anyway. You all have a good time, and I'll see you this evening."

They were going to her parents' for dinner that evening after having lunch with Gabe's parents. Lydia was going to be so full at the end of the day she might not be able to waddle home.

"Okay," she said, reaching out again to give him another hug. "I'll see you then." She hugged him tighter than usual as she added, "Thank you. For everything."

He was smiling in his typical dry way as they pulled apart, and they were walking toward the door when Ellie came racing down. "Uncle Thomas!" she exclaimed on seeing him. "Merry Christmas."

She gave him a hug like they were long-lost friends, and she and Lydia went out to the porch to wave Thomas off as he drove away.

Gabe was coming down as they returned, and some sort of internal radar pointed him immediately to the cinnamon rolls. Ellie took hers enthusiastically, but she groaned as they brewed themselves coffee to go with them.

When they were done eating, she demanded that it was finally time for presents and there couldn't possibly be any more delays.

Ellie had many more presents than Gabe and Lydia, so she got to open hers first. She was ecstatic over all the books and clothes and toys, and the necklace with a book pendant that Lydia had picked out for her was a definite hit.

Then it was Lydia's turn to open presents. Ellie had picked out a necklace for her too—a pretty heart on a chain. She'd also gotten Lydia a fantasy book series that the girl assured her she would absolutely love. Gabe got her books on jewelry making to help with her ideas about work for the rescued women. And he'd gotten her lovely, soft pajamas with cars on them—"since you asked so nicely the other night," he explained with a grin. And he'd gotten her a pair of earrings that were nicer than any jewelry she currently possessed except her engagement ring.

She loved her gifts, but she was almost more excited about Gabe opening his.

"Open mine first," Ellie insisted, plopping a box on his lap that was wrapped with more enthusiasm than skill.

Gabe made a big deal about slowly unwrapping the paper until Ellie was squirming with excitement.

Then he gasped as he opened the top to reveal the blue tie with books on it. "It's amazing," he said, picking it up. "How did you possibly find it?"

"We looked forever," she admitted, giving Lydia a little smile. "But I knew exactly what I wanted to get for you."

"I can't believe you found something so perfect." He reached over to give the girl a hug. "Thank you so much. I'll wear it on Sunday."

"Oh, and you have to open this now too," Lydia said, handing him a small box.

Gabe gave her a curious look, and she was barely holding back laughter as he opened it with raised eyebrows.

Inside was a tie clip with a sculpted pile of books on it.

Ellie squealed with delight. "It's perfect! It goes with the tie!"

Gabe burst into laughter as Ellie moved over to hug Lydia, and Lydia decided her present was a resounding success.

After a while, Ellie brought her hoard of books upstairs to organize them on her bookshelves, and Lydia scooted over toward Gabe on the couch. His eyes were soft when he looked at her.

"I have another present for you," she murmured huskily.

He arched his eyebrows. "And when do I get it?"

"Tonight. It's not fit for mixed company."

A certain smolder ignited in his eyes. "I see."

"I have something for you to wear and something for me, but they're both presents for you."

"I have a feeling I'm going to like yours better than mine."

She laughed and kissed him, just to the side of his mouth. "You probably will."

"I don't suppose there's any chance of a nap sometime earlier today," he said, stroking down her back toward her hip.

"I doubt it, between visits to your parents and mine. We'll have to wait."

He made a guttural sound. "Now I'm going to be thinking about it all day."

"Not around your parents, surely."

"Hopefully not."

"Well, I can't wait to see you in your present. And you know that patience isn't my virtue."

"When it comes to you," he said, meeting her eyes with a deep, hot look, "it's not my virtue either."

He pulled her into a kiss, and they were still kissing when a voice came from the entrance to the room. "Are you kissing again?"

"Maybe a little," Gabe said, pulling away from Lydia's mouth and smiling toward his daughter. "But she's my wife, so I'm allowed."

"I guess so. But this isn't kissing time. This is family time. Isn't it?" Ellie didn't look upset or grouchy as she came over to the couch to sit with them. She looked like she was laughing.

"Yes, it's family time," Gabe agreed. "But a few kisses are allowed during family time."

Gabe and Ellie continued on with an extended conversation about how much kissing was acceptable during family time, but Lydia was only half listening.

Mostly she was thinking that this morning was the first time in her marriage when she felt like she was part of this family—wholly, completely, no more questions or hesitations. She was theirs as much as they were hers.

ABOUT NOELLE ADAMS

Noelle handwrote her first romance novel in a spiral-bound notebook when she was twelve, and she hasn't stopped writing since. She has lived in eight different states and currently resides in Virginia, where she writes full time, reads any book she can get her hands on, and offers tribute to a very spoiled cocker spaniel.

She loves travel, art, history, and ice cream. After spending far too many years of her life in graduate school, she has decided to reorient her priorities and focus on writing contemporary romances. For more information, please check out her website: noelle-adams.com.

35029210R00125